MADDY YIP'S

GUIDE TO PARTIES

**LOOK OUT FOR MORE
IN THIS SERIES!**

**Maddy Yip's
Guide to Life**

**Maddy Yip's
Guide to Holidays**

MADDY YIP'S

GUIDE TO PARTIES

STORY and
PICTURES by
**Sue
Cheung**

ANDERSEN PRESS

First published in Great Britain in 2023 by
Andersen Press Limited
20 Vauxhall Bridge Road, London SW1V 2SA, UK
Vijverlaan 48, 3062 HL Rotterdam, Nederland
www.andersenpress.co.uk

2 4 6 8 10 9 7 5 3 1

British Library Cataloguing in Publication Data available.

ISBN 978 1 83913 312 1

Printed and bound in Great Britain by Clays Ltd,
Elcograf S.p.A.

To my brothers and sister.
There's a bit of you all in this book
and that's what makes it funny.

THE LAUS

Timmy (future Olympic gymnast)

THE CHANS

The best cooks in Plunkthorpe

KAYLA DIGBY

No way is Jack going out with an intellectual!

JANINE JANGLE

The human glitterball TV presenter

GED SPONGER

Eating MY chocolate

while crushing a brick into dust

EVIL TWINS

Ted is the one with the snot

We'll be good

Honest

(Don't be fooled)

HEENA

(DEV'S LITTLE SISTER)

TOOTY-TOOOOOT-TOOTY-TOOOOOO OOT!!!

Tuesday

Tuesday is the **WORST** day of the week and here are the reasons why:

    1. It is even more **'MEH'** than Monday

    2. There are twenty-four *billion* hours in
       a Tuesday

    3. I have P.E. with Ged **'BULLY'** Sponger

    4. It's Mam's **'HEALTHY DINNER'** day (barf)

Another reason: this morning, I opened the kitchen window to let a moth out, **FUZZFACE** saw it, leaped onto the draining board and knocked over the pans that Dad had **STACKED LIKE JENGA**. It might as well have been an armadillo in a cymbal shop.

'Nice one, nut,' said Jack, slow clapping at the table.

ARGH!

'YEAH, NICE ONE, NUT,' Oli repeated, sniggering into his Ricicle Krisps.

Jack is my older brother and Oli is the little one. Both are **total berks**. For a start, I have grown out of that dumb '*nut*' nickname, which refers to an **UNFORTUNATE** incident of a dry roasted peanut being stuck up my nostril, a **VERY** long time ago. And also, this mess was equally the cat's/Dad's fault.

Me and Dad were gathering up the pans when Mam rushed in, scanning the room like a **sniper**. She is always on high alert due to being childminder of the evil Tatlock toddlers, who if left unattended are more **DESTRUCTIVE** than erm . . . yes, an armadillo in a cymbal shop.

'**What was that?**' she said.

'The mad animal,' I told her.

'Which one? There's four of you, five, including Hulk,' Dad quipped.

We heard a **crash** behind us. The moth, which was still flapping about, must have landed on the swing bin lid, because the stupid moggy had fallen in, then scrambled out,

leaving a trail of
burst teabags and
mouldy yoghurt
pawprints.

Rarwl!

Mam groaned. 'I think I will sign up for those yoga classes I saw online. I could do with some **peace and relaxation**.'

Then she did something not so relaxing, which was to rummage through the kitchen drawers, while swearing under her breath. **'I need to check when I can go first. Where's my diary?!'** she shouted. Quickly realising her aim was to be calm, she said softly, 'I mean . . . did any of you happen to have come across my diary?'

'What the hell's this?!'

WHIRRR

She held up a gadget and got all shouty again.

'It's my **MOTORISED iCE-CREAM CONE**,' said Jack.

OMG, Jack is so bone idle he can't even be bothered to revolve his ice cream with his hand.

'Wish I'd invented that,' Dad said approvingly.

Mam raked around some more. **'And this?'**

'That's my **CHORK**,' said Oli. 'It's got a fork on one end and chopsticks on the other. Don't need it now I can use chopsticks.'

'I think you'll find that picking up food by stabbing it repeatedly is *not* the correct way,' I informed him.

Mam sighed loudly. **'Help find my diary, please. I need to find dates for yoga, so I can get away from you lot!'**

By that point, we were more eager than Mam for her to go to yoga so WE could get some peace. Plus, by swapping it for her usual boxing classes, she'll hopefully go off the idea of getting a punch bag hung in the living room. A second later, Oli came running into the kitchen with the diary. '**FOUND IT!** Well, actually, Luke found it in the garden with his quantum-powered swivel-eyes.' (**Luke Skywalker** is Oli's action doll and BFF.)

7

'The **obvious place**, of course,' Mam answered, sarcastically. She held the diary up by one corner. **'Looks like it's been run over by a lawnmower!'**

'Oh yeah,' mumbled Jack. 'I thought the grass was a bit **LuMPY** when Dad asked me to mow it the other day.'

Mam shook bits of grass out of it and tutted. Just when we thought she was happy at last, she stopped at a page and cried out, **'OH NO!'**

'What's up now?' said Dad.

I hoped it was a **TOAD iNNARDS** squashed between the pages.

'It's Agung's **eightieth** birthday in a few weeks and I totally forgot. I was going to do a party, but time's a bit tight now.'

'Ah poodle ploppage!' said Dad. He doesn't do grown-up swearing like Mam. **'I forgot too.'**

Agung, which means Grandad in Chinese, is Dad's dad, so he shouldn't have forgotten.

I butted in, 'But it's his **eightieth**. He's got to have an epic party, to match his epic age.'

'Why don't we have a little one instead?' said Mam. 'Just us lot, with a Chinese takeaway.'

UGH.

Then the doorbell rang. I opened the door and **FUZZFACE** sprinted in, terrified. The dreaded Tatlock twins were coming down the path with their dad. Within a nanosecond of Mr Tatlock leaving, Ted had tipped the cat's breakfast over Tod's head, making him bawl. This was my cue to expertly slope out of the front door and escape to my best mate Dev's before I pushed them both face first into the **STEWED KiDNEY SLOP**.

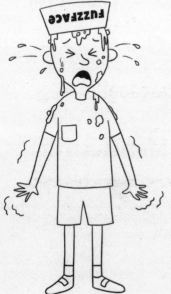

Dev was waiting outside his house when I got there. He never ceases to amaze me with his unending wardrobe of **BiZARRENESS**. Today he was wearing a raincoat which appeared to have been fashioned out of a coral reef-themed shower curtain. 'Hey, you're not my friend, you're my *anemone*!' I joked. Dev gave me a weird look. 'You know, sea anemone, *enemy*, geddit?' He didn't. Then I spent the whole walk to school feeling seasick while telling him about Agung's birthday.

'Party extravaganzaaaaa!' he sang.

He goes to drama club so he is unnecessarily over-the-top.

'Don't get too excited,' I said. 'My mam and dad don't have time to sort a party.'

Dev frowned and thought for a moment. 'I know, why don't *you* organise it then, and I'll help?'

HMM, I guessed my parents wouldn't need much persuading. After all, me and Dev did take **DITZHEAD** Oli and **BUMBLING** Agung away for a weekend to Sudmouth and brought us all back alive.

'You might be *wearing* fish, Dev, but right now, you deffo don't have the brain of one!' I replied. 'That's an **ACE IDEA**. I mean, how hard can it be to organise a party?'

'**Let's do it!**' said Dev, doing a double twirl with a jazz hands flourish.

'OK, but first I need to convince my parents that we are highly proficient **PARTY PLANNING EXTRAORDINAIRES** – no pressure!'

How to convince people you're up to the job

By teatime, I was still struggling to come up with anything that might persuade Mam and Dad to let me and Dev plan a party. **THEN I HAD A THOUGHT.** Why not ask the main man himself? It was his birthday, and he was sensible enough to make his own decisions. I found him in his converted garage room wearing a pair of swimming shorts and knee-high wellies.

MAYBE I WAS WRONG.

He was watching a repeat of his favourite TV show, STRICTLY BALLROOM PRANCING. The human glitterball presenter flounced on and shouted out her well-known cheesy catchphrase, 'It's time to put on your prancing shoes and PAAAARRRTTy!!'

'Party!' Agung said, pointing at the telly.

'Yes, and hopefully you'll get one too,' I told him, even though he hadn't a clue what I was going on about.

At tea, I pretended to like Mam's quinoa casserole and said nicely, 'You know how you were saying that Agung's birthday's coming up?'

'Yep, looking forward to my chop suey,' said Dad.

'Why don't we ask Agung what *he* wants? It's *his* birthday.'

'YEAH, ASK HIM. I WANNA PARTY!' Oli yelled.

Dad looked at Mam and Mam rolled her eyes.

I carried on, 'If he wants one, me and Dev can organise it. It'll be nowt compared to the Sudmouth trip last month, and that was a major undertaking **WORTHY OF A KNIGHTHOOD**.'

Mam and Dad didn't look sure. Agung doesn't know much English (he speaks a

Chinese dialect called Hakka), but he recognised the words birthday and party. He nudged Dad and said something to him excitedly. (Dad is the only one in our family to speak Chinese). Eventually Dad turned to us and said, **'Agung's up for it.'**

'Well, if he wants a party and Maddy's in charge,' Mam said, 'that means I've more time for de-stressing. OK then, why not?'

I pumped my fist. **'YESSSS!'**

'You better stick to my budget though,' said Dad, probably working out the precise amount for a platter of **SOGGY SANDWICHES** and a bottle of pop.

'**Sorted!**' said Mam, happy that someone else was in charge. 'And I'm sure Jack and Oli would love to give Maddy a hand, wouldn't you?'

NOOOOO!! It was only meant to be me and Dev!

Oli shot his hand up, forgetting that he wasn't at school and that Mam wasn't his teacher. '**BAGSY I DO THE INVITES!**'

'Good lad,' said Dad. 'What about you, Jack?'

Jack looked like someone had just slapped him in the face with a **WET HADDOCK**, then weirdly, he smiled and replied, 'Sure. Maddy will need some expert management anyway.'

HUH! Maybe he should manage his **GREASY ZITS** first.

Anyway, **HURRAH** for me! (Oh, and Dev), because we were about to make this party go down in Plunkthorpe history.

Wednesday

I couldn't wait to tell Dev. I thought about texting him last night, but this news deserved a real life high five. Plus, Mam had trapped me in her bedroom for hours while she tried on a billion **Lycra outfits** and asked which looked the most appropriate for yoga. **I DUNNO!** The closest I've ever got to yoga is when I slipped on a froghurt in the shopping centre and landed in the splits!

As predicted, Dev was more excited about what he was going to wear at the do than the actual organising. I knew because he showed me the **sparkly** jumpsuits and **sequinned** blazers in his AGUNG'S 80TH BIRTHDAY PARTY OUTFIT IDEAS sketchbook. I reminded him that it would be helpful to have a venue and guests first and he replied, '**Excuse me,** but if I want to make a jumpsuit, it takes **five days** for the **crinkle satin** to arrive.'

EXCELLENT.

I grabbed his pad and wrote down:

AGUNG'S 80TH BIRTHDAY PARTY TO-DO LIST (18 days to organise!)

diamond detail

Then underneath I added:

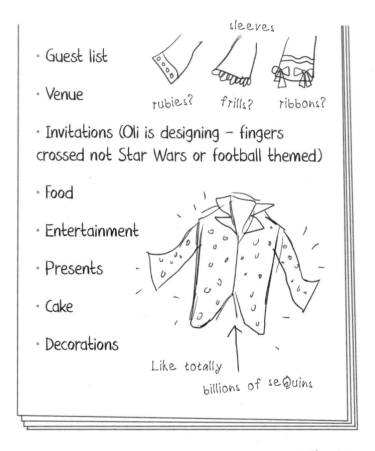

- Guest list
- Venue
- Invitations (Oli is designing - fingers crossed not Star Wars or football themed)
- Food
- Entertainment
- Presents
- Cake
- Decorations

sleeves

rubies?   frills?   ribbons?

Like totally billions of seQuins

Dev read it and raised an eyebrow. **'That's quite a lot of stuff.'**

Yeee-ahhh. The list *had* turned out longer than I thought, but hey, nothing we couldn't handle.

At morning break, we started planning.

'Let's do pressies first, that'll be well easy,' Dev said.

I racked my brains, 'Arthritis cream . . . compression socks . . . dried figs?'

'Remind me never to invite you to my eightieth!' Dev scoffed.

But I couldn't think of anything else apart from **FLATULENCE TABLETS** for his atrocious wind (Agung's, not Dev's). Old people are hard to buy for, because no matter how lavish your gifts, they will always be most ecstatic over a bag of wine gums. We decided to get some ideas from our classmates by asking what their grandparents got for their birthdays. The results were as follows:

1. **Elsie Thadani's nan** = a year's subscription to *Cottage Upholstery Stuffing* magazine

2. **Liv Hall's gran** = a seaweed spotting boat trip around the Shetlands

3. **Tom Wrigley's pops** = a luxury toupee, which ended up in the trifle

None of the suggestions helped as they were either **RIDICULOUS**, **BONKERS** or just plain **DAFT**.

25

We carried on brainstorming at Dev's after school. Halfway through, Dev's little sister, Heena, **BURST** in to show us her new dance routine (a mini-Dev in the making, **LORD HELP US!**) Dev told her to shimmy her way back out of the door and she started **WAILING**. If she was anything like Oli, she would have gone running to her parents with some **OUTRAGEOUS** story about how we dangled her out of the window by her ankles, so I said, 'Oh, go on, let her, it won't take long and it's free entertainment.'

Look at me, everyone!

WOOF!

WOOF!

Dev's dog, Graham

As Heena was skipping about with her **glittery** dress on, it sparked an idea which made me **SHRIEK** and **JUMP UP** off the bed. Heena must have thought I'd seen a giant spider because she **SCREAMED** and **SCARPERED** out of the room. Well, that was another way to get rid of her, I guess.

'Listen,' I said to Dev. 'You know that dancing competition on the telly you like, full of people with **OOMPA-LOOMPA** coloured fake tans?'

'You mean **STRICTLY BALLROOM PRANCING**?'

'Yeah, Agung is a total fanboy.'

Swish

'Cos he has **excellent taste**, like moi,' said Dev, flicking his fringe.

'What's that bit at the end of the show where the host with all that blusher on her face turns up at people's houses?' I asked.

'That's **Surprise a Prancer**. People write in and nominate fans of the show, then Janine Jangle, who I HEART, surprises them with a visit.'

I waited for Dev to click.

It took the same amount of time as a flea to climb Mount Everest.

'I get it!' he finally blurted. 'We should write in and get Janine to visit Agung.'

'FINALLY, SHERLOCK!' I sighed.

'That would be awesomesauce!'

'Yes, but even *better* . . . '

Then I explained how instead of writing a letter, we could do a VIDEO! Something that would blow Janine's mind. Then on it, we'd tell her about Agung's **eightieth** coming up and how he is Prancing's biggest superfan. It was such a brilliant idea that we started on the script straight away. We got stuck when it came to why Agung was such a fan though, because all he did was watch religiously each week, just like anyone else did. In the end we had to exaggerate and put stuff like:

'Agung has a duvet cover with your face printed on it.' (Actually, it's a tea stain, but the same colour as her fake tan!).

'Agung has made up his own Prancing jiggly shoulder dance.' (Actually, he does this whenever he's in a good mood anyway).

The script was looking ace, but Dev said he could **zhuzh** it up even more.

'Instead of just talking, I could dance on it too. Then there's no way they'd turn us down ... plus, one of **Prancing's** talent spotters might see me and book me as a **Star Prancer!'**

Apparently, a **Star Prancer** is a special guest dancer. I should have known there was something in it for Dev. He was right though; it would get us noticed! We start making the video tomorrow.

How to ZHUZH up a video

Dancing

Ribbons

Glitter

Falling over

Bog roll

Sand

When I got home, I was telling Oli about our **Prancing** idea when Jack appeared, sticking his big spotty conk in. **'What's going on?'** he asked, stuffing *CROCODILE CRUNCHIES* into his gob and spraying crumbs everywhere.

I told him about our video message and he commented, **'Good work, keep it up.'** Call that managing? Managing to be a complete cretin, if you ask me!

On my way back downstairs, I walked past Jack's door and heard him talking to someone on the phone. '. . . So, I thought, why not make a video message and send it off to **STRICTLY BALLROOM PRANCING?'**

THE TOERAG!

'Yes, yes, I came up with it all by myself,' he boasted.

ARRRGH.

'The party is going to be amazing. Of course, I'll send you an invite, pronto!'

WHAT. A. GIT.

There could only have been one person he was creeping to . . . Kayla Digby. The girl in his year from school he's been chasing forever. Well, it *will* be forever because there's no way an intellectual like Kayla would ever be associated with a div like Jack. Last week, he **WAXED HiS MONOBROW** in an effort to impress her. As if *that* would make a difference. He needs a whole head transplant! I was about to charge into his room, grab his phone and ram it down his sneaky throat when I thought, no. I would wait and get my own back in good time.

Tonight, Mam made corn on the cob, buckwheat breadsticks and chunky chickpea dip, and it wasn't even 'healthy dinner' day – **YUCK!** As I was yanking bits out of my molars and nursing my sore jaw from chewing so hard, Agung tapped me on the shoulder and said something in Chinese. He pointed at his plate and I saw that his **FALSE GNASHERS** had got caught on his cob. They were grinning at me so I laughed out loud and choked on a kernel. Then I spilled a glass of dandelion and burdock on my top trying to wash it down in a panic. **'Stop mucking about!'** said Mam, which I thought was very inconsiderate, seeing as I clearly needed urgent medical attention and she was the one who tried to kill me in the first place.

After Jack **WHACKED** me hard on the back (because, any excuse) and I coughed out the kernel, the whole ordeal got me thinking about the party food. I had to make sure it was **FALSE TEETH FRIENDLY** and not a choke hazard, because even though I wanted a *killer party*, I didn't mean in THAT way! A second later, Dad walked in, took one look at our tea and put a pizza in the oven for himself.

'Hey, Dad, can you ask Agung what sort of food he'd like at his party,' I croaked.

'Good idea,' Mam replied, unclamping his gnashers from the cob and rinsing them under the tap. She gave them back to Agung, who could now make himself understood.

Dad and Agung talked in Chinese then Dad translated. 'He says he'd like the Chans to cook a buffet including hoisin duck pancakes, beansprout noodles and char siu.' I wasn't arguing with that! Also, the Chans are Agung's second cousins who run the BAMBOO GARDEN Chinese takeaway on the high street, so they are bound to do us a good deal.

'And don't forget the birthday cake,' Dad added.

'OH YEAH,' I said. 'I know, let's get him a novelty one!'

'That's exactly what I was about to say,' said Jack. 'Two great minds and all that.'

WHAT?! He is going to PAY for hijacking my ideas!

Thursday

Woke up this morning in a **MILD PANIC**. I must remember to move **AGUNG'S 80TH BIRTHDAY PARTY TO-DO LIST** from the wall, where it is the first thing that stares me in the face, and replace it with a relaxing picture of a wombat drinking banana milkshake on a deck chair. I can't be starting my day all **STRESSED OUT**. I might turn into a **HEALTH FREAK** like Mam!

As usual, I took Agung his morning cup of

oolong tea and was surprised to find that his room, which is normally **ORGANISED CHAOS**, was just **CHAOS**. Instead of storage boxes being stacked against the wall, they were sprawled about in the middle of the room with stuff spilling out, mainly tat that Agung hadn't bothered unpacking since moving over from Hong Kong a few years ago. Among the ornaments and photos was a pinkish upside-down mixing bowl, which I thought was odd. Then it moved and I realised it was Agung's baldy head.

Shiny bonce

PHOTOS

PHOTOS

'WHAT ARE YOU DOING?' I said.

He looked up at me with a packet of sun-dried shrimps in his hand and answered, 'Eh?'

I did my normal bad sign language by POINTING AIMLESSLY, SHRUGGING and GRIMACING (my normal look basically), and Agung explained something in Chinese, which I took to mean two possible things:

a) 'I've been looking for these sun-dried shrimps.'

b) 'I've been looking for a sun-dried shoe.'

Shrimp and shoe sound similar in Hakka ('har' and 'hai'), and it was entirely possible for a **CRUSTY SANDAL** to be hiding in that pile of junk. He waved me over and I had to scramble across several bin bags. By the looks of it, he was having a clear-out. Agung took my hand, mysteriously placed a COin in my palm – a Chinese one with a square hole in the middle – and said something with the words, 'hao dor' in it. I am mega unreliable at keeping stuff safe, so I gave it back.

'No, you keep!' said Agung, pushing the COin into my hand.

He was quite persistent so I took it.

Back in the kitchen, I showed Jack the coin. Maybe he would know more about it despite being an utter plonker.

'Don't you know what that is?' he snarked.

'No, that's why I'm asking – duh.'

'It's a Chinese cash coin, stupid. **They're lucky charms,**' he shouted, leaving the room.

Oh good. Hopefully I'll be lucky enough to see Jack drown in a pit of yak saliva one day . . . I mean, **SOON**.

Then Dad came in to put the kettle on.

'What does 'hao dor' mean in Hakka?' I asked him.

'It means, "a lot",' he replied.

WOW! Maybe Agung was trying to tell me the coin is worth loads of money. **LUCKY AND PRICELESS – BONUS!** After the party's over, I will treat me and Dev to a shopping spree down at the **NINETY-NINE PENCE SHOP**. To keep the special coin super safe, I threaded string through the hole, tied fifty-seven knots, superglued some Sellotape around the knots and wore it around my neck under a massive woolly scarf, **JUST IN CASE**.

How to keep your VALUABLES safe

Place valuables in thick metal box

MARSH MALLOWS

Weld on lid

(burp)

Feed box to shark

Send shark to moon

During morning break me and Dev started writing the script for the *STRICTLY BALLROOM PRANCING* video. Dev was in pure admiration of my out-of-season scarf look. He said it was a '*cutting edge fashion statement*', but I told him it was for security reasons and that I was actually sweating like a pig in a sauna. I gave him a peek of the COIN.

'It's a lucky charm worth loads,' I said, and he replied, 'Well, it doesn't go with that scarf, I can tell you that for nowt.'

GREAT.

When I read the finished script, I noticed that I only appeared for a couple of lines. Somehow Dev had managed to take over the rest with ten dance routines and eighteen costume changes. The lad was out of control! I scribbled some out and rewrote it so that we had the **equal** parts that an **equal** partnership **should** have. By then I was overheating, so I had to take my scarf off.

Suddenly, Dev squeaked and whispered, **'Watch out, plonker about.'**

Ged Sponger stomped over.

PFFT! *HAR! HAR!*

'**Whassat?**' he said, grabbing the script.

He read it and laughed out loud. I was offended that he had found my deadly serious piece of quality showbiz writing funny.

'**Where's yer sweets?**' he said.

'**IN MY BELLY, YOU BIG . . . BLOATY-FACED . . . BERK!**'

I'm not sure where that came from, but I immediately regretted it.

Ged fumed. I thought he was going to smash my skull in with his **HUGE HAMMY FiST**, but then he spotted the COiN around my neck. **'I'll have that!'** he growled. There was no way I was going to let Sponger's **GREASY SAVELOY FiNGERS** anywhere near it. I willed the COiN to exude its magical luckiness (or however it worked) and explode Ged's eyeballs out or set his lughole hairs alight, then Mr Ginsberg, the history teacher, came past – **PHEW!**

'Ah, a Chinese cash coin,' he said, completely oblivious to the fact that I was about to get pulverised. 'Could be worth a *pretty penny*, s'cuse the pun,' he tittered.

HUH! If only his lessons were so amusing! As he walked off, Ged smirked and muttered,

'**Worth a few quid, eh?**' Then clomped off to plan his next assault on me.

After tea, I went to Dev's to start shooting the Pʀᴀɴᴄɪɴɢ video. It was better to use his room as Oli said he wanted to use mine as a party invitation design studio. Mrs Sharma gave us some old **sparkly** sari material to hang up on the walls and I drew the curtains. Not for atmosphere, but so that Mr Pike, the **GRUMPY OLD CODGER** who lives between me and Dev, couldn't see what we were up to. Heena demanded to be in the video too, but she got her foot caught in one of the saris and fell onto Dev's homemade **tin foil tiara** and squashed it. Dev collapsed into an over-acted sobbing heap and sent her out. It was a small price to pay to get her out of the way.

Mr Sharma is very good with technical stuff and has lots of up-to-date equipment (up-to-date until the nineteen nineties, that is). He let us borrow his camera and tripod to film with. I decided to do it Janine Jangle style because she has exactly the same accent as us:

ME: It's time to put on your prancing shoes and PAAAARRRTYY!! Hi, Janine Jangle, we're making this *Surprise a Prancer* video to nominate Agung, my dear old . . . **GRAHAM!**

Dev's dog, Graham, put me off by scratching at the door. I wanted to do that bit again but Dev was 'in the zone' and made me carry on.

ME: Soz, I meant *grandad*! Agung turns **eighty** soon. He's Prancing's biggest fan, tunes in every week and also watches the repeats on repeat.

[Dev enters screen from left, wearing a *frilly salsa blouson*. He does a quadruple pirouette and staggers off DiZZiLY to the right.]

ME: **Fact:** Agung has your face printed on his duvet. **Fact:** Agung has invented his own Prancing dance.

[Dev enters screen from right doing the Agung shoulder jiggle. Meanwhile, Graham has broken into the room and starts grappling with his leg warmers. Dev tries to shoo him off but ends up hobbling off screen with the dog clamped to his ankle. Graham is taken outside, where he barks. **Loudly.**]

ME: If Agung had not been cruelly afflicted with bunions, his ambition was to appear on your show.

[Dev appears with walking stick (broom handle) to demonstrate Agung's bunion-racked hobble.]

ME: So he would be made up if you could come and surprise him on his birthday!

[Dev spins the stick, which promptly whacks his shin. He hobbles off again.]

ME & DEV TOGETHER (extreme close-up): We hope you've enjoyed this video as much as we've enjoyed making it!

Which was a total lie, as the only bit I enjoyed was Graham **mauling** Dev. At the end I added, 'Please respond with utmost urgency. Thanks in advance.'

I thought the video perfectly highlighted our skills as **COMEDY GENiUSES**. But Dev wanted to edit out Graham and all my **BLOOPERS**, so he could appear professional and potentially be picked as a Star Prancer. I'm not sure anyone could be classed as professional wearing a squashed tin foil tiara, but what do I know about showbiz?

Friday

Life had suddenly become very **HECTIC**. I don't like hectic. I like lying on the sofa and staring at the ceiling for hours on end, cuddling a family pack of **CROCODILE CRUNCHIES** to myself, preferably **PICKLED ONION**. Today after school, I had planned to go to the baker's to order Agung's birthday cake, but I hadn't even thought about it yet! I was sure it should be a novelty one though, because:

55

a) Agung loves odd things . . . like himself,
   or his socks

b) It could become a 'thing' and I might get
   one for my birthday next

c) It would be a good back-up surprise in case
   STRICTLY BALLROOM PRANCING
   falls through

At morning break, I grabbed Dev and we
thought of cake ideas.

'What's your gramps into?' asked Dev.

'For a start, Plunkthorpe Bird of Prey Centre.'

Dev gasped, 'What about a cake the shape of

an eagle then? They're
huge and magnificent.'

'We're on my dad's
budget, remember?'

'Eagle nest?'
Dev suggested.

'BUDGET.'

'Eagle chick?'

'BUDGET.'

Humph

'All right, just
do a **piddly** egg
then,' he sulked.

57

'We could probably afford that,' I half joked.

Then I remembered, I could buy *any* cake I liked. I pointed to the COiN around my neck.

'HEY, I'LL BE MINTED WHEN I SELL THIS. LET'S GO WITH THE EAGLE!'

YAY! My idea! My idea!

'YAY! My idea! My idea!' sang Dev, doing a can-can high kick. Then we high fived and missed as usual.

When home time bell went, me and Dev met at the gate and made our way to the baker's at the end of the high street. I'd spent all day lying low because Ged was still on a mission to murder me after I called him a **big bloaty-faced berk**. Plus, he was after my coin. Dev offered to be my bodyguard, which was nice, but he couldn't fight his way out of a **WET SHEET OF BOG ROLL**. Instead, I summoned the *magical* forces of my lucky coin by rubbing it three times (because it's always three in fairy stories etc) and got ready to insert a blunt pencil up Ged's nose in case that failed.

Thankfully we got to the baker's undetected, but it looked like the whole of Plunkthorpe was queueing up. Maybe it was the **END OF THE WORLD** and everybody was stockpiling, but then I saw the **Two-for-one baps** sign by the front door. Us Plunkthorpians do love a bargain. When we eventually got served, I couldn't hear with all the

old biddies arguing over bap quotas per person, and the lady behind the counter was FRAZZLED.

'WE WANT A CAKE THAT LOOKS LIKE THIS,' I said, holding up my phone.

'Sorry, we don't sell sponge puddings.'

I looked at the screen and realised I'd accidentally shown her a zoomed-in photo I'd taken of Jack's **NECK BOIL** when he wasn't looking. I grimaced and quickly scrolled to get the picture of the eagle I saved earlier, but I couldn't find it and the biddies behind us were getting impatient.

'**You're holding up the queue,**' the lady whinged.

'WE WANT AN EAGLE-SHAPED BIRTHDAY CAKE,' I explained, over the din.

FRAZZLED bakery lady wrote the details in the

order book so fast it looked like a chimp with boxing gloves on had done it in hieroglyphics. She told us when it would be ready for collection then turned to serve the next customer. It was all a **BIT RUSHED** but she must have known what she was doing, she'd been working in the baker's ever since bread was invented.

As I was saying bye to Dev at his house, Mrs Sharma appeared at the door and cried, **'I MUST COMPLIMENT YOU ON YOUR STRICTLY BALLROOM PRANCING VIDEO.'**

Dev must have shown it to her.

'Thanks, Mrs S. Which bit did you like best?' I was interested to get an outsider's opinion.

'Most definitely my saris hanging on the wall. They make the whole thing look so **blingy**. Nice touch and well done to me.'

FANTASTIC.

Then she asked if they were invited to the party and I got a sudden cold sweat on. **Horror of horrors**, I'd forgotten about the guest list! 'Yes, course you are,' I bumbled. 'I just haven't got round to it yet.'

Dev, who is supposed to be my loyal project partner and trusted bezzie, gawped at me and cried, **'What, you haven't told anybody about the party?!'**

'Yes, all right, thank you very much for reminding me but I would be grateful if you didn't rub my face in it right now if you don't mind!' I muttered, through gritted teeth. 'As a matter of fact, it's my next job.'

Mrs Sharma frowned. 'Party planning is **HARD** work. Rather you than me,' she said, unhelpfully. Then to make my job list even longer, she added, 'Why don't you **SURPRISE YOUR GRANDAD** by inviting some of his family from overseas? We always love our relatives coming to visit, don't we, Dev?' Dev nodded enthusiastically. **THANKS, DEV.** No way did I want extra work, but after it sunk in, I thought it might be a good back-up surprise in case anything happened to the cake back-up surprise, that was in turn the present back-up surprise.

No one was about when I got home. Jack was at Gav's and Dad was tinkering about in the shed making some MAD INVENTION birthday gift for Agung. Agung was at the bingo with Mam (he doesn't play, he just likes the scampi in a basket they do, and also wreaks **havoc** with the rest of the players by shouting 'House!' for a laugh whenever he feels like it). That meant I could sneak into his room and see if I could find his address book.

I had to barge the door open as I forgot Agung was in the middle of a clear-out and there were boxes everywhere. I would need help ploughing through it all – SOMEONE SKINNY and FERRET-LiKE. I went back into the hallway and shouted up the stairs, **'OLI!'**

Oli came bounding down like a dog hearing the word 'walkies'.

I said to him, 'I've never known anyone with such **FOMO**. You know . . . **F-O-M-O**?'

Oli scrunched his face and replied, 'Fear . . . Of . . . Mushy Onions? Yes, you're right, I *do*!'

GAWD.

'NO, OLI, FEAR OF MISSING OUT,' I sighed. 'Anyway, listen, I'm doing something extremely top secret and ultra-important and I think Luke's swivelling eyeballs could help.'

Oli sprang back upstairs to fetch his best friend doll. When he returned, he barked,

'REPORTING FOR DUTY, SIR. WHAT IS OUR MISSION?'

I told Oli my plan to invite Agung's Hong Kong relatives to the party and that he was to scale the heights of **JUNK MOUNTAIN** in his room and look for anything that resembled an address book.

'AND TRY NOT TO BREAK ANYTHING,'

I said. 'Apart from the record of being the dorkiest brother alive, which you already hold.'

He gaped and a little bit of **DRIBBLE** fell out of the corner of his mouth. I couldn't bear to look at him any longer, so I sent him to work on the multi-drawer sideboard. That would keep him out of my hair for a while.

I rubbed my **coin** and waded through Agung's pile of junk. At this rate, I'd end up raiding skips like Dad! I unearthed three bird guidebooks, two pairs of binoculars and a random toilet brush before I saw a notebook underneath a stack of empty Cup Noodle pots on Agung's bedside. **YESSS, THE COIN WORKED!** There were loads of addresses in the notebook, but only one in English, which was good because it meant less work.

It read:　　Mr & Mrs Lau
112a Harbour Walkways
Koolung Town
Hong Kong
Email: hello@lausmail.hk

I've heard Dad mention them a few times. I think they are Agung's third cousins twice removed or something equally baffling. **'OLI, YOU CAN STOP NOW,'** I shouted across the room. But he didn't reply as he was too busy sniffing a sun-dried shrimp. I copied the address onto a scrap of paper then went upstairs and rewarded myself with a lie-down and four caramel wafers. I couldn't see any evidence of Oli's party invites though. Maybe he has finished already and will astound me with his incredible masterpieces soon.

AGUNG'S 80TH BIRTHDAY PARTY TO-DO LIST

- Guest list (will email Laus asap)

- Venue (need to find)

- Invitations (soon to be astounded)

- Food (Agung wants Chinese buffet, will ask Chans)

- Entertainment (have left Dev in charge — help!)

- Presents (remind Dev to send Prancer video)

- Cake — DONE (Yesss!)

- Decorations (??)

Saturday - two weeks till PARTY!

I went to thank Mrs Sharma for her **TOP TIP** and told her that I was going to follow her advice and ask some Hong Kong relatives to Agung's party as a surprise.

'He will be **VERY** happy. You'd better be quick though, his birthday is **SOON**,' she said.

I groaned. 'I was going to message them on Jacks's email last night, but he was using our laptop for a school project on salamanders.'

More like messaging Kayla to tell her how amazingly the party he is single-handedly organising on his own is coming along! Which reminds me, I still have to get him back for that.

'You can use my email if you like,' said Mrs Sharma, handing over her phone.

'AH, TA!'

I passed it to Dev so that he could type while I dictated, but was slightly **DISTURBED** to find his hands decked out in black fingerless gloves and a fake gold signet ring.

'The focus is on fingers this week,' he said.

'**GOOD,**' I replied. 'Then focus your fingers on this keypad while I tell you what to write.'

He **TUTTED** and **POISED** in readiness. I didn't have the foggiest how to go about writing a letter to an adult I'd never met before but I guessed it had to be polite and formal, like **posh** people in nineteenth-century costume dramas.

'**RIGHT, HERE GOES** . . . ' I started.

Dearest Mr Lau,

I hope this correspondence finds you in good health. I believe you are a relative of Mr Yip, formerly from Koolung, Hong Kong, now residing in Plunkthorpe, North East England.

Luck has it that I stumbled (literally, over several bin bags) across your email address, so it is with good fortune that I write to ask if you would like to attend his eightieth birthday party, of which the date is Saturday 21st May of this present year.

I realise that is quite soon, so please be accepting of my apologies for the short notice.

76

Here's hoping that you will grace us with your presence (and presents!). It would be a marvellous surprise indeed for him to see you (that's if he remembers to put his specs on, lol).

RSVP, ASAP, PDQ, YOLO

Yours wholly sincerely,

Mr Yip's granddaughter, Maddy, eleven years old (but very mature for my age)

P.S. I am writing from my bezzie mate's mam's phone, which is why I'm showing up as Mrs Sharma.

Dev **CACKLED** rudely at the 'mature' bit and went on about using words like 'lit' and 'fam' instead of 'old-fashioned drivel'. But before he could protest any more, I leaned over the phone, pressed 'send' and that little task was over with – **HOORAY!**

While we were on the phone, Dev decided at long last to show me the final edited version of the **STRICTLY BALLROOM PRANCING** video he had sent to his mam. He had removed the best bit where Graham breaks into the room and clamps onto his ankles, which was a shame. I am certain Janine would have said yes without a moment's hesitation if she'd witnessed that **comedy gold**. But anyway, it would have to do as we needed to get a shift on. Dev did a quick search for **Prancing's**

applications email address and sent it off. Then I joined him in an **EXCITABLE** jig, except he was dead good and I just looked like I was trying to fend off an *angry* porcupine.

How to do an excitable jig

Dev told me he was skipping drama club today, to work on party entertainment ideas.

Then it struck me – the drama club would be an **EXCELLENT VENUE**! We decided to see if Miss Gabb, the club manager, was around and would be up for it.

'It's all yours,' she said, when I asked to borrow the club for the day. I knew she'd let us because she owed us **infinite** favours since me and Dev organised a recent variety show fundraiser to save the club from closing down. So, the venue was sorted double quick. **RESULT!**

As soon as we got back to Dev's, he messaged Prancing on his mam's email again, to tell them where they needed to show up for the birthday party. A moment later a message **pinged** in from the Laus!

'WHAT'S IT SAY?' I said, snatching the phone off him.

I clicked the email and cleared my throat . . .

Dear Maddy,

Thank you for the kind invitation to your grandad's 80th birthday celebrations, which we accept with great enthusiasm. We are indeed distant cousins of your grandad and lived on the same street. He and my parents used to swap bags of rice and pak choi.

My wife and I have always wanted to visit England. We are big fans of European history and can't wait to view the splendid cobbled

streets, thatched cottages and ancient forts. My son Timmy, who is seven, is also excited to see a real castle for the first time! I've been given special permission from his school to let him have time off to attend this special family occasion.

You will be pleased to hear that I have already bought our plane tickets and we'll arrive in a week. We look forward to surprising your grandad with our visit. Please forward your address and telephone number.

Yours sincerely,

Mr Lau

YESSSSS!!!

I was gagging to tell Agung when I got home because keeping secrets for me is like keeping a bag of marshmallows under the bed – it's not long before they're out the bag **(HAR, HAR!)**. Instead, I had to be content with just telling Mam and Dad. They would be more than impressed by what I'd done.

Dad was busy making Mam's tofu lasagne recipe **(YUCK)**. There was a bowl of something nicer next to him, so I stuck my finger in and tasted it.

'**That's my home spa beetroot face pack by the way,**' said Mam, breezing past.

BARF.

After I tried not to vomit and scraped the offending goo out of my mouth, I spluttered, 'I've got something to tell you, which is **OUT OF THIS WORLD!**'

Jack walked in and commented flatly, '**Please** let it be that you've been accepted into the Mars colonisation programme and will be away for **a very long time**.'

HA! Once I'd told Mam and Dad about my latest party win, there was no way Jack could pass this one off as his own. Oli suddenly appeared from nowhere, eager to hear what I had to say. He couldn't care less most of the time, but when it sounds like there might be gossip, he is like a fly around a festering cow pat. As soon as everyone was in the kitchen (apart from Agung, who was safely in his room looking for his specs – probably a good thing as tofu lasagne is best unseen), I announced, **'SO, HERE'S MY NEWS.'**

'Get on with it then,' Jack moaned.

'I've invited some **VERY SPECIAL** people to the party.'

Oli put his hand up and yelled, **'YEAH, AND I KNOW WHO!'**

85

I gave him a Mam-style glare to stop him blurting it out.

'That's nice, love, who?' said Mam, stirring her face pack.

'THE LAUS, AGUNG'S RELATIVES FROM HONG KONG.'

'Oh really? That's great!' said Dad. 'Where are they staying?'

I hadn't thought about that, but was sure we could find space in our house.

'ER . . . HERE?' I suggested.

'**WHAT?!**' screamed Mam, flinging her hands up in horror and splatting a glob of beetroot face pack into Oli's eye. 'But we don't have room for guests . . . and **look at the state of the place!**'

SPLAT!

Jack folded his arms and sat back **SMUGLY** in his chair while I got a roasting. Oli kept quiet, either because he was temporarily blinded, or because he didn't want to be blamed as my accomplice. By now, Mam had lost the power of speech, so Dad took over.

'And . . . um . . . when exactly are they coming?'

'NEXT WEEK.'

My voice came out like a mouse being run over by a bulldozer.

Mam stared at the wall blankly and mumbled, 'I think I'll do the Tibetan chanting class too after yoga tomorrow.'

'Don't worry, we'll get it sorted,' said Dad, with a look on his face that blatantly said **'HELP.'**

'First class, nut,' quipped Jack.

It was **BEDLAM** and all because I tried to be helpful.

Friday - a week later

THE LAUS ARRIVE TOMORROW!

I have spent the last few days helping Dad clear Agung's rubbish so they can stay in his room. Jack's been 'flexing his mind' at Kayla's book club when he should have been flexing his puny muscles shifting boxes. Oli hasn't helped either. His excuse was a footballing injury, which on closer inspection, turned out to be a microscopic **HANGNAIL**. And Agung, whose junk it is in the first place, has been hiding in the living room, gluing **STINKING** bird feathers into a scrapbook. When Mam came back from her first yoga class, she showed us how to do a headstand and promptly fell on our neatly stacked boxes and trashed the place again. **SO MUCH FOR FAMILY SUPPORT!**

Agung will be staying in Jack's room temporarily, while Jack kips on a mattress on his floor. I hope Agung **snores** and **FARTS** extra loud while he's in there – **HAR HAR!**

Later on, Dad drove us to the **BAMBOO GARDEN** to borrow a fold-up guest bed to put in Agung's room for the Laus' little lad. It was a good time to ask the Chans about party food.

'**Hey, nice to see you!**' Mr Chan shouted, over the deafening clatter of a wok. He was tossing noodles without spilling any, which is a very cool skill. I was going to ask if I could have a go, but their walls probably looked better without my noodly modern art splattered all over them.

HOW TO TOSS A WOK

Small circular motions ✓

Do NOT attempt to flip like pancake! ✗

Mrs Chan squeezed my arm. She has the grip of a **SiLVERBACK MOUNTAiN GORiLLA**. 'You are skinny like stick insect,' she said.

'Mam's making us eat healthy at the moment,' I informed her.

'A growing girl like you need more food,' said Mrs Chan, shoving a bag of prawn crackers in my hand. I'm not sure about growing as I have not exceeded four foot six during the past two years. But I wasn't disagreeing to the 'more food' bit. I showed my appreciation by inhaling the entire bag of crackers in ten seconds and let out a little burp. I felt bad asking them to do the party food after they'd just given me free snacks and lent us a bed, but it had to be done. I rubbed my lucky coin and was just about to open my mouth when Mr Chan brought up the subject.

'You are good girl organising Agung's party. We're looking forward to it. Who's doing the catering?'

I was so relieved he'd mentioned it first that I blurted out, **'YOU ARE!'**

I thought I'd blown it because there was an ultra-long silence. Then I realised Mr Chan had got out his calculator. 'Of course, for your grandad we do **anything,**' he said, tapping away on it. 'And we give you fifty per cent off for bulk order.'

PHEW.

'You're a legend!' Dad grinned, doing a quick mental calculation of the savings.

'No lobster dumpling though,' said Mrs Chan. 'Because is too expensive.'

'WHATEVER YOU CAN DO WILL BE AMAZING, THANKS!' I said, hugging her, then gasped for breath as she crushed me back.

Well, that was another task crossed off the list. Not only that but we left with five portions of special fried rice and three tubs of sweet and sour sauce, which makes up for tofu lasagne a gazillion times over.

After tea, Dev called. I thought he was going to tell me that STRICTLY BALLROOM PRANCING had watched our video, recognised our outstanding talent and hired us as producers, but it was about the entertainment. He said that Princess Silvia Gomez Kumquat (real name Maureen Snodgrass) from his drama club had been bugging him for a gig at our party. She is just as desperate as Dev to become *a star* and will do anything for free to kick start her career. I told Dev, 'She only does songs from *Les Misérables* and they make you want to stick your head in a bucket and bang it repeatedly with a rolling pin.'

'Still not as depressing as your dad's budget,' Dev replied, quite rightly.

Anyway, I had the guest list to sort out.

AGUNG'S 80TH BIRTHDAY PARTY GUEST LIST

- The Chans (x2)

- The Sharmas (x4)

- The Tatlocks (x4 – UGH to Evil Twins, but Mam wants to keep Mr and Mrs Tatlock happy, as they are her best-paying customers)

- Members of Agung's birdwatching club (x10)

- The Laus (x3)

I was adding up the number of guests when Jack blundered past and knocked into me on purpose.

'What you doing?' he said.

THE CHEEK! He had not lifted a finger, yet was sticking his **PiMPLE-RiDDLED SCHNOZZ** in at every opportunity.

'The guest list, if you must know.'

'Oh yeah?' he said, pulling up a chair.

GREAT.

He leaned over to have a look and I recoiled at the **PUSTULE** on his left nostril.

'You've missed out Kayla,' he said, prodding at my list.

It took all my willpower not to stab his spot with my compass. 'I'm not sure Dad's budget will stretch to an extra guest,' I replied coolly.

'Then I'll just have to tell Mam it was me who helped you get eighty per cent for your science homework last week.'

'**WHAT?**' I gasped. 'I paid you three packets of **CROCODILE CRUNCHIES** and a chocolate éclair for **ONE** question!'

I *was* desperate at the time. I rubbed the coin and waited for Jack's zit to grow tentacles and take over his entire face. Instead, he breathed on his nails and polished them on his shirt, waiting expectantly.

'OK, *fine*,' I said. 'Now please kindly remove your **ugly** mug.'

He patted my head and walked off, the **PATRONISING PILLOCK**. I was still going to get him back for pretending to organise everything.

Including us lot, there were twenty-nine

people going to the party. Getting the invites out was **top priority**, so I ran straight upstairs to grab them off Oli. I couldn't wait to inspect the finished handiwork.

'Hey, Oli, giz us the invites,' I said.

Oli was lounging on the bed with **FUZZFACE**, reading a comic. He clearly looked like someone who had finished their task yonks ago and was now treating themselves to a well-earned rest.

Oli looked at me **gormlessly** and replied, **'WHAT, NOW?'**

'If you could provide the invites **immediately**, that would be most convenient,' I snapped.

'You never said *when*,' he whimpered.

AMAZING.

TRUE, maybe I should have given him a deadline to finish by. But he'd had almost a fortnight to scrawl whatever blasted design he wanted on those things, and they still hadn't been finished! I should have known better than to leave a DUNDERHEAD alone with this job.

'How far have you got then?' I asked, **exasperated**. I figured I could at least send whatever he'd done.

Oli opened his bedside drawer and revealed a stack of completely untouched, blank white cards.

WHAT?!!

I AM SURROUNDED BY IMBECILES!

'Look, Oli, if it was Christmas and I'd asked for a snowdrift design, we could probably have got away with it, but right now we need **BIRTHDAY** invites!'

The almost bursting veins in my temples made Oli jump off the bed, grab his felt-tips and start scribbling for dear life. I had to have a little lie-down to get over the trauma.

Just then, Mam came in, chanting mystical words and wafting a **PONGY** essential oil diffuser. She saw Oli slaving away with his stack of cards and uttered, 'Gosh, looks like someone could do with these relaxing chamomile vapours.' Then she turned and spotted me lying spreadeagled on the bed and shrieked, '**Maddy!** I can't believe you're leaving your poor little brother to make all those the invites on his own, while you lie there like **Lady Muck**!'

She dragged me off the bed by the duvet until I landed in a heap on the floor. Nice to see the relaxing vapours are having the desired effect on Mam.

After being winded and getting my breath back, I got up to help Oli. Not only would the job get done that way, I could make sure he wasn't going to cover them with collages of C-3PO or something. I had to deliver them tomorrow first thing, so we stayed up till half ten to finish the job.

CORRECTION . . . *I* stayed up till half ten, because Oli fell asleep at a quarter to eight. He was **DRiBBLiNG** on top of the finished invites and making the felt-tip run, so I had to forcefully remove him. In the end, the design was a rushed **eighty** in purple bubble numbers, outlined with a leaky, green glitter pen. They looked superb actually. If you happened to be in a dimly lit room wearing a blindfold.

Saturday - one week till PARTY!

Did not sleep a wink due to a disturbing nightmare I had about a giant **eighty** purple bubble number chasing me down the street with an axe! Thankfully, I now have a picture of a wombat drinking banana milkshake on a deckchair on my wall, so I stared at that all night to take my mind off it.

The Laus would be arriving later, so I had to get the invites delivered before they got here.

I thought about borrowing Oli's bike to speed things up, but felt too tired to pedal. I decided to bribe Jack into helping me out. It was the least he could do considering he was supposed to be 'managing' the party organising. I found him in the bathroom 'managing' his hair with stupid styling gel instead. I stood between him and the mirror and waved an invite in his face. **'CAN YOU GIVE ME A BACKIE ON YOUR BIKE?'**

'Move or you're dead!' he bellowed.

'I need to deliver this to Kayla's.'

I KNEW IT. As soon as I mentioned the word *Kayla*, Jack dropped everything and was all ears.

'Yeah, sure!'

It took him approximately zero seconds to sprint out to the back garden, pull the tarpaulin off his mountain bike and shout, **'Get a flippin' move on, then!'** Any excuse for him to stalk the poor girl.

When we got to Kayla's house, no one was in. Jack looked gutted.

'I guess you'll see her at the party,' I said.

I needed to keep him sweet, as I was about to break the news about delivering the rest of the invites in my bag that I **accidentally-on-purpose** forgot to mention.

111

He put the invite back in his pocket.

'She needs to say *yes* first,' he grumbled.

Cor, I am glad I'm not suffering from teenage hormones. It must be miserable being a **LOVESICK, ZIT-INFESTED, BUM-FLUFFED-CHIN BORE** like Jack. It didn't take long for us to deliver the other invites though, because he was cycling in such a *rage*.

Back at the house, Mam was in a *rage* of her own. She was rushing from one room to the other with a lavender aromatherapy spray in an attempt to 'Create an atmosphere of stillness.' I'm sure it would be very still, after she'd suffocated us all to death!

Then she nearly fell over Oli, who was chasing Hulk, his scabby guinea pig. Hulk used to belong to Oli's school, but they gave him away after he kept escaping from his cage. (It's Oli that needs a cage if you ask me.) When the doorbell went, Mam screeched, **'It's them! It's them!'** as if we hadn't a clue.

Look, yummy doughnut!

Dad answered the door and there were the Laus. When they saw us, their jaws dropped. We were all coughing our guts up from the lavender fumes and just at that moment, Oli dived on Hulk in the hallway.

Finally, Dad stopped choking and croaked, **'Welcome to Plunkthorpe!'** Somehow, I don't think the Laus were expecting *this*. I saw the Laus' **posh** taxi pull away and wondered how loaded they must be to afford a lift from the airport in it. When I sell my lucky coin, I will hire a **posh** taxi to take me and Dev for a shopping spree down at the **NINETY-NINE PENCE SHOP.**

Mr Lau shook Dad's hand. 'Great to meet you, **at last**.'

He spoke **DEAD GOOD** English and there were no buttons missing off his shirt like Dad's. Compared to Mam, Mrs Lau was very smart too. 'How rude of us to leave you standing on the doorstep. Do come in,' said Mam, in that weird voice she normally uses for Mr and Mrs Tatlock.

Then the Laus' son, Timmy, barged into the hallway. He was almost identical to Oli; except he wasn't dressed in *Barry's Bargain Basement* clobber.

'I'm going to be an Olympic gymnast!' he yelled.

Mam and Jack helped lug the Laus' ten (!) suitcases in while Timmy somersaulted up and down on the sofa like a wallaby with a flea infestation. I'm not sure about Mam, but Oli was well impressed. Dad appeared with a tray of **posh** cups, saucers and teapot, which I never even knew we owned.

'How **adorably** British,' said Mrs Lau.

How **ADORABLY STINGY** of Dad to use our best crockery once a decade, more like!

'Maddy, *go fetch your grandad*,' said Mam.

Agung still hadn't a clue the Laus were coming. It was the longest I had ever kept a secret. Though it also helped that we hardly understand a word of what each other was saying. I went upstairs and heard, 'It's time to put on your prancing shoes and PAAAARRRTTy!!'

So I knew Agung was watching STRICTLY BALLROOM PRANCING repeats on Jack's portable telly. (Wish the PRANCING people would put on *their* PRANCING SHOES and get back with an answer). I interrupted his chair dancing by waving at him to follow me while pointing frantically at the door, but the silly buffoon thought I was copying his dancing, so I had to go over and prise him out of his chair.

Maximise limb flapping...

...in the middle of dance floor

He hobbled down the stairs at the speed of an **ARTHRITIC TORTOISE** and I wondered if by the time we made it to the bottom, the Laus would still be there and hadn't had to catch their return flight back to Hong Kong. Agung walked into the living room but instead of gasping with delight like I expected, he looked **befuddled**. Then I realised he didn't have his specs on so I had to dash back to get them. After I plonked them on his face, he managed to focus. 'Ahhh,' he cooed. Then he said something in Chinese and Dad and the Laus laughed.

'He asked if they'd brought any pak choi,' said Dad.

'No pak choi, I'm afraid,' chuckled Mr Lau. 'But we've brought some other gifts.'

'I got a medieval knight from the airport shop!' Timmy shouted, waving his plastic figure at Oli. Everyone else got these:

Oli – Animatronic Grogu (could this be the end of BFF **Luke Skywalker**?)

Jack – Skincare set (word must have got around about his zits, ha ha!)

Dad – Silk tie (he doesn't even know how to wear one!)

Mam – Pair of silk slippers (perfect for relaxing in)

Agung – Laughing Buddha carved out of jade (looks just like him)

Me – AN ABACUS?!

If only the Laus knew how much I loathed:

a) maths

b) maths-related tools

c) people who like maths and

d) how the word 'maths' even sounds

'JUST WHAT I'VE ALWAYS WANTED!'

I said, trying to be sincere but just sounding really sarcastic.

After everyone except me fussed over their gifts, Dad served dinner. When he put the plates on the table, the room went quiet.

'Is everything all right?' he asked.

'Well, um, we were just expecting something more *British*,' said Mrs Lau.

'But spaghetti Bolognese has been a British classic since the 1970s,' Dad replied, crestfallen.

'Oh, that's . . . interesting,' said Mr Lau, baffled.

Come to think of it, why *is* an Italian dish a British classic? It made me wonder what the other classic British dishes are. Dev might know.

After dinner, Dad showed the Laus where they would be staying in Agung's **NiFTY** garage conversion. I had taken extra care to stack the empty Cup Noodle pots on the sideboard neatly by flavour order and opened the window earlier to let the joss stick fumes out. Mr and Mrs Lau didn't seem too overjoyed by my efforts when they walked in and saw the place though. Especially Mrs Lau, whose eyes had a look of dread in them when she saw Agung's **LuMPY** mattress.

Dad, completely unaware, swept his hand around the room like a hotel concierge and said, 'I know, we're **really** spoiling you, aren't we?'

Timmy pushed past me, climbed onto the fold-up bed and started hopping about on it. The bed started making alarming **squeaking noises**, so I tried to stop him but the flimsy hinges gave in after the fifth bounce and the bed collapsed like a clam shell, sandwiching Timmy inside. All that was left of him was a left foot poking out. Mrs Lau tried not to faint while Dad and Mr Lau ran to his aid and pulled him out, **DAZED** and **DISHEVELLED**.

'Sorry about that,' Dad cringed, examining the hinge and scratching his head.

'GREAT GYMNASTICS THOUGH!'

I cried, trying to lighten things up.

Nobody laughed. I hoped Timmy wasn't as broken as the bed.

Just as me and Dad were about to leave them in peace to unpack and acquaint themselves with the **YIP MADHOUSE**, Mam waltzed in, spraying a gallon of vile lavender aromatherapy fragrance in everyone's faces. **'Sweet dreams, everyone!'** she chirped.

BRILLIANT.

Sunday - early morning

Dad woke me up **clattering** about in his shed at five past six this morning, the MANIAC. He's been faffing around for days trying to make a gift for Agung's **eightieth**. I don't know why he doesn't just buy it from the **NINETY-NINE PENCE SHOP** like he does with everybody else's birthday presents. I keep meaning to ask what he's making, but I don't fancy a lecture on circuits and semiconductors at the moment.

I went downstairs to make toast and was surprised to find the Laus already up and dressed in the kitchen. I was embarrassed about the table being a **MESS** as I'd been making party decorations the night before and hadn't bothered clearing up. I was brushing the bits of card and glitter onto the floor, when Dad **crashed** in through the back door and **bashed** his toolbox down, making the table look even worse. **'Morning all! Did you sleep all right?'**

'Marvellous,' whimpered Mrs Lau, fishing glitter out of her drink.

'Only a little bit of jetlag,' Mr Lau said.

They were gulping coffee out of pint glasses and had bags under their eyes the size of **CAMPING HAMMOCKS**, so I suspected they were being polite.

Then Timmy shouted out, 'I didn't, Mr Yip! My bed was hard, the room **smelled funny** and I've got a **headache** from all that **noise** you were making in the shed!'

Everyone looked **mortified**, except for me. I was ready to settle down with a bag of popcorn to watch the morning's entertainment.

'Well, there was that too,' said Mr Lau, awkwardly.

'So, I hope you don't mind,' Mrs Lau added. 'But we've booked Plunkthorpe Park Hotel for the rest of our stay.'

Ooh, I've heard that packets of honey roasted cashews come free with their rooms –

UTTER LUXURY! When I sell my lucky coin, I will hire a **posh** taxi to take me and Dev for a shopping spree down at the **NINETY-NINE PENCE SHOP**, then a stay at Plunkthorpe Park Hotel so we can sample their prestige complimentary snacks.

Mr Lau said, 'Agung can have his room back then, and we can all be comfortable.'

Apart from me, who will still have to put up with Dad's unsociable D.I.Y.

'Sorry about that,' said Dad. 'Tell you what, let me take you out for a slap-up English breakfast to make up for it . . . and for last night's spag Bol.'

Just then Mam, who had missed all the drama, walked in and remarked, 'Great idea, and we can show you some historical landmarks along the way.'

The only historical landmark I could think of was the pothole in the high street that the council's been meaning to fix for years. I'm sure it was the last thing the Laus wanted to see after a terrible night's sleep.

'That would be lovely,' said Mrs Lau. 'We've only ever seen stately homes on television before.'

'And castles!' yelled Timmy.

Like most tourists, they must have watched

one too many episodes of *Pride and Prejudice* and *Great Expectations*. In our town, they were better off having no expectations. Cross fingers Dad had a scenic route planned, so their illusions weren't shattered.

Jack shuffled into the kitchen looking as crumpled as the Laus. Agung must have done me proud with his **thunderous** snoring and kept him up all night – serves the cretin right, HA!

Oli and Agung were nowhere to be seen, so Mam made me go and fetch them. Oli was still flat out, so I woke him up using my trusty **PiLLOW BASHiNG** method. Agung was up and had managed to put one trouser leg on before being distracted by a wood pigeon building a nest in the tree outside. When I eventually herded them downstairs, Dad rattled his keys and rapped cringely, **'I'm a man with a van and a very cool plan!'**

He was in charge of the work minivan this week, so we all crammed in and set off. Dad drove through the nice part of town, full of detached houses with hanging baskets, double garages and doormats that said **Welcome** on them. It was a good move as the Laus would be fooled into thinking Plunkthorpe was like that all over. It is also where Jack's pretend girlfriend, Kayla Digby, lives, so he perked up when he thought he might see her. The excitement didn't last long though, as the road was closed off due to construction works. Dad diverted left, which was the worst idea, because now we were in the run-down estates.

I acted quickly as we cruised past an empty park with a lone plastic carrier bag blowing across the playground. **'THIS IS THE THRIVING COMMUNITY HUB!'** I blared. 'And this is the nature conservation area,' I went on, pointing to a fox dragging a sack of mouldy cabbages out of an upturned wheelie bin.

Dad tried to help me out with my disastrous guided tour. 'Here on your right is the town hall,' he joined in. 'A municipal building made entirely from reinforced concrete.' **WOW.** Never mind jet lag. If he carried on like that, we'd all be in a coma.

We were going past a crumbling public toilet and a giant wall of graffiti when Mrs Lau piped up, **'That looks charming.'** She pointed at a big Victorian house on a corner. I didn't mean to add to the list of atrocities Plunkthorpe had to offer, but as usual my humungous mouth took over and I yelled out, **'THAT'S THE WITCH'S HOUSE!'**

How to recognise a WITCH'S HOUSE

Snarling wolf's head knocker on door

Overgrown weeds and creepy crawlies in garden

Windows covered in dust, cobwebs and ivy

Cauldron instead of pond

If Mam could have reached me from the passenger seat, I swear she would have throttled me there and then. I forgot we were supposed to be making Plunkthorpe look like something out of a Jane Austen novel. Mam forced a smile and commented, 'It's actually one of the town's nicest features.'

Timmy trembled. 'Why is it called the witch's house?'

I was always taught to tell the truth, so I did: 'Because even though there's never anyone in, the lights go on and off at night and sometimes you can hear ghostly "**wOOOOO**" noises.'

Timmy's mouth dropped open, then Oli screamed.

137

'Congratulations, nut,' Jack drawled.

I changed the subject by pointing to the next building, 'Look, it's the Plunkthorpe Bird of Prey Centre!'

Agung said something excitedly in Chinese. Dad replied and Agung frowned. He probably wanted to go in, but Dad couldn't afford it because our **extravagant** brekkie was going to cost a fortune.

Finally, we parked up and Dad said to the Laus, 'You wanted *real* British cuisine? Well, you're in for a surprise.' Yep, and it sure wasn't going to be one of the pleasant varieties either – because we had stopped outside the suspiciously cheap and not very cheerful **Mildred's Cafe**.

FANTASTIC.

As we sat down, the server bowled over and whacked down a pile of dog-eared menus. 'This is what we call a **"greasy spoon"**,' said Dad, proudly.

Timmy picked up his spoon, noticed the oily smears and shouted, **'Yes, you're right, it is!'**

And Oli nearly passed out laughing.

Dad ordered the full English breakfast for everyone and the Laus both surprised and disgusted me by asking for second helpings of black pudding – **YUCK!**

As we left the cafe, Kayla was walking past with a friend. Jack dashed over like a **DAFT WHIPPET** and pulled an envelope out of his pocket. It was Kayla's party invitation that he hadn't posted as he wanted to deliver it in person. I could just make out what he was saying: 'I made them all myself.'

THE LYING PILLOCK!

'I'm impressed by the amount of work you're putting into this party,' said Kayla.

Jack shrugged. 'I could easily take more on.'

'More on'?! **HE IS A MORON, MORE LIKE!**

Kayla took the card out and stared at the embarrassingly wonky purple 'eighty' bubble number outlined in squiggly green glitter that I had hurriedly plonked together while rushing to get them finished.

Jack looked mortified. He wasn't expecting the design to be so amateur. **TOO LATE.** He had admitted to being the artist.

'Oh, it's er . . . very *expressionist*,' Kayla stuttered.

'Thanks!' Jack replied, wincing. Then he ran off to hide in the minivan. **HAR HAR!**

Sunday - late morning

When we got home, Mam pointed out the nearest stately home on a map, so Mr and Mrs Lau could go for a visit and fulfil their **WILDEST DREAMS**. Agung was going along too with his binoculars, to do some bird spotting. While Mam walked them to the bus stop, I went to find out what **MIND-BLOWING** invention Dad was making for Agung's birthday.

I could hardly see him when I walked into

143

the shed as he was surrounded by heaps of Cup Noodle pots.

'Is this Agung's pressie, a year's supply of his favourite snacks?' I asked.

'Better than that,' Dad replied, polishing a metal box covered in buttons. '*This* is a portable Cup Noodle maker!'

But making a Cup Noodle only required four steps, which Agung was perfectly capable of performing himself:

1) Peel off lid
2) Pour in water
3) Stir
4) Scoff

DUH.

'**Stand back and prepare to be amazed,**' said Dad.

Prepare to be scalded by a face full of boiling hot noodles, more like, I thought. I went and stood outside, safely shielded by the door and peeked through the thinnest sliver of a gap. Dad placed a Cup Noodle under a nozzle and pressed a button. The cup filled with hot water, then a fork popped out and stirred the contents about before **splattering** them into a bowl.

'**Watch, this is the best bit!**' Dad shouted, prodding another button.

A spout appeared and out **squirted** a tonne of hot chilli sauce. It would have been the best bit if most of it hadn't landed on Dad's shoes.

'As you can see, a few things need repositioning,' he muttered.

The whole thing needed repositioning, if you asked me – **INTO THE BIN!** He'd spent ages on it though so I told him, 'Well, it's unique. That's for sure.'

Back inside, Mam heard me going past the living room and immediately shouted, **'Maddy, can you take Oli and Timmy to the park for some fresh air while I practise my tree poses?!'**

UGH, why doesn't she take them to the park herself? She could get practice with actual trees then. And why does she never ask Jack? We all know he's playing **Ninja Banana 2** when he claims to be doing homework. I was about to object but realised that **BRAT-SITTING** was miles better than watching Mam crashing about into furniture. She's not a natural yogi, I have to say **(BUT NEVER TO HER FACE)**.

'OKAAAAY THEN,' I huffed. I could hear thumping about in my bedroom and wondered if Timmy was in the middle of wrecking my bed, so I ran upstairs and flung open the door. Oli and Timmy froze when they saw me. They were both in strange positions on the floor, looking flushed.

'OK, WHAT WERE YOU DOING?'

I asked.

'Timmy's showing me his knight's suit of armour,' said Oli, innocently.

His hair was sticking up and he only had one sock on (Oli, not the knight). He was being **EXTREMELY WEIRD** (more so than usual if that is at all possible).

I got them to put on their shoes and just as I was shoving them out of the door, Mam shouted out, **'And don't let them get into trouble, do you hear me?'**

AS IF I WOULD.

I stopped off at Dev's to see if he wanted to come. When he clocked that there were two kids in tow, he said, 'Double the trouble, double the price. It'll cost you a twin-pack of custard tarts.' **THE CHEEK.** Last month I kept an eye on Heena while his nail polish dried and I only got three sherbet pips for it!

On the way to the shop, we were so engrossed by Timmy's demonstration of his medieval knight's hinged visor that we failed to notice Ged the plonker trundling around the corner. I went to rub the COIN for luck but it got stuck under my jumper.

'Oi, Yip, giz your coin!' Ged barked.

'BOG OFF, BLOATY FACE!' I said, assuming a **KARATE POSITION** but just looking like the Tin Man from *The Wizard of Oz*.

Oli went to defend me by thrusting Luke's three-inch lightsaber at Ged. Timmy did the same with his knight's two-and-a-half-inch sword.

It seemed to do the trick as Ged turned his attention to Dev's beaded man bag. **'What's in there?'** Panicked, Dev handed it over and I tried not to crease up as Ged pulled out a nail file, a hairband and a **DEBONY DELITE** from *Girlzlife* keyring.

Then Ged plucked out
an envelope **'Dosh?'**
he grunted.

'That's my party invite!' spluttered
Dev, trying to snatch it back.

TOO LATE. Ged opened it up and read it.

'All-you-can-eat Chinese buffet? I'm up for
that,' said Ged, shoving the invite in his pocket.

Just as we thought he was about to leave;
he **LUNGED** towards me and grabbed the string
with my coin from around my neck. I tugged it
off him and it **snapped**, catapulting the coin
over my head. Then we both turned to see it
disappear into a bunch of weeds behind a railing.

EXCELLENT.

'Now that was silly, weren't it?' Ged sneered and off he clomped triumphantly.

ARGH! An infinite multitude of **NINETY-NINE PENCE SHOP** sprees was lying in those weeds somewhere.

Dev grabbed my sleeve and pointed to the weeds.

'Oh my god. You know where this garden belongs to?'

I squinted through the railings.

'THE WITCH'S HOUSE!' we both cried.

'I'd rather shave off my eyebrow hairs and eat them in a sandwich than go in there,' I said.

'I'll do it,' Timmy declared.

'BUT AREN'T YOU SCARED OF THE WITCH?' said Oli.

'I'll only be going in the garden, not the house. And I'll get through these railings easy with my double-jointed gymnast limbs,' he boasted, puffing out his chest and star-jumping.

I did a swift comparison of the space in between each railing and the width of Timmy's **ginormous** head. No chance. But before I could stop him, Timmy shoved his bonce through the gap. Just as with the fold-up bed incident, I was a millisecond too late and his head was instantly jammed.

(GULP)

'Ighhh ewww hughhh!' he squealed.

'Yes, you are an unbelievable simpleton,' I agreed.

'Cripes, what do we do now?' Dev whispered loudly.

'I'M TELLING MAM!' snivelled Oli.

'Shut up, **BLABBERMOUTH**, I'm trying to think,' I said. 'What about we pull him out?'

'I say push,' said Dev.

I imagined Timmy being shredded like a joint of bacon in a slicer. It wasn't a good look.

'Ighhh ewww hughhh!' Timmy protested.

'If we don't get you out, we are in *big* trouble,' I said to him.

'Less of the WE,' Dev interrupted. 'I was dragged into this. I am an innocent bystander.'

I WAS SERIOUSLY BEGINNING TO QUESTION OUR FRIENDSHIP.

In desperation I ran to the door of the house and knocked, hoping the witch might have a spell that could bend iron . . . or heads. There was no answer, so I got out my mobile and dialled the emergency services.

Five minutes later, a fire engine arrived. They are quick in Plunkthorpe, as they only usually deal with chip pan fires and pets up drainpipes. I explained what happened to the chief fire officer and nearly fainted when he told the crew to fetch a chainsaw. **HOW WOULD I EXPLAIN TIMMY'S MISSING PARTS TO HIS PARENTS?!**

How to extract bonce from railings

Loads of oil (olive is healthiest)

Headshrinking powder (if it exists)

Get elephant to headbutt out

Chainsaw (for bars, not neck!)

We waited for Timmy's screams as the railings were cut off around his scrawny neck, but it was over surprisingly quickly and Timmy remained unscathed.

'This is the most exciting thing that's happened to me, ever!'
he yelled.

The fire chief walked us home to report back to our parents. Mam looked like she was going to kill me 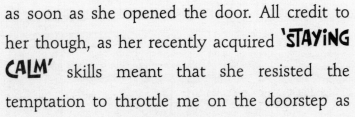 as soon as she opened the door. All credit to her though, as her recently acquired 'STAYING CALM' skills meant that she resisted the temptation to throttle me on the doorstep as she listened to the chief explain the situation. As soon as he left, Mam shrieked, '**I leave you alone for FIVE minutes and the entire Plunkthorpe fire service ends up at my house, not to mention an almost mutilated child!**'

SHE DOESN'T HALF EXAGGERATE.

'Go and apologise to the owners of the house for having their railings cut, and fetch that coin back. It belongs to your grandad.'

Well, technically it didn't any more but I didn't want to argue with her in that state. Then I remembered the witch hadn't answered her door.

'THERE'S NO ONE IN,' I said.

159

'You'll just have to wait there till they come back in, won't you?' she barked.

Me and Dev left the two brats at home and made our way back to the scary house. I thought about sneaking through the hole in the railings, but if we'd have been caught trespassing, we'd have the police involved as well as the fire brigade, not to mention what sort of nasty curse the witch would cast on us! Instead, we played **ROCK, PAPER, SCISSORS**, to see which mug got to knock on the door, and I lost – because I didn't have my lucky coin on me, OBVS! I crept up the stone steps and tapped the snarling **wolf's head knocker** as lightly as I could. I could hear footsteps getting louder and louder behind the door. Then the key rattled in the dusty keyhole.

AGGGHHH!!

THE WITCH WAS IN!!

I sprinted away, nearly knocking Dev over, then we both stumbled back to his in order to comfort eat a shedload of marshmallows and forget it ever happened.

Sunday - afternoon

The Laus and Agung returned from their day out just as I got back from Dev's, so Mam didn't get the chance to ask how my trip to the witch's house went. I think she was more concerned about how to tell the Laus about Timmy's **BONKERS BONCE** incident. Turns out she couldn't get a word in edgeways as they were busy listing every boring, minute detail about the stately home, which took forever.

'We had a tour around the stables, the landscaped gardens and the double-height vaulted ceilinged ballroom,' said Mrs Lau.

It was all right for them to be **GALLIVANTING** around, while I was left to figure out how to prise their twit of a son's head out from a pair of iron bars without slicing his ears/nose/eyelids off.

'It was **splendid** to see a grade one listed property from the eighteenth century in real life,' Mr Lau said. 'Especially one with major collections of oil paintings and sculptures.'

I tried not to yawn as they named every person in the portrait paintings hung on the walls. I wondered if Agung had found it interesting, then I noticed he was chomping on a box of luxury salted caramel truffles and knew that must have made his day.

'Look, here's us with the King,' said Mr Lau, showing us a picture on his phone.

Wait, what? **THAT WAS IMPOSSIBLE!** I had a closer look at the photo.

'Oh, it's you standing next to his portrait,' I said.

The Laus laughed. 'Well, we're not likely to meet anyone famous around here in real life, are we?'

Oli and Timmy puffed downstairs. They were both wearing sweatbands and red in the face. **WEIRDOS.** Before Mam could explain, Timmy ran over to his parents and said something to them in Chinese. The Laus looked *horrified*. I was certain he was telling them about mine, Dev and Mam's combined first-class childminding skills. Then Timmy turned to Oli and said, 'It was brilliant when the fire engine turned up wasn't it?'

'YEAH,' Oli giggled.

Mrs Lau **BRISKLY** inspected Timmy's head and when she was certain there wasn't any damage, she said, 'Well, despite the unfortunate incident, I'm glad you had your own little adventure.'

PHEW!

Timmy had conveniently left out the part about the chainsaw.

As if Plunkthorpe didn't pose enough dangers, Mam suggested that the Laus take Timmy to the seaside at Sudmouth tomorrow. She has never been and so remains unaware of the **giant killer seagulls** and vomit-inducing roller coaster rides. I hope the Laus don't end up booking the dodgy bed and breakfast we stayed in either. Mind you, they would probably think that olive green bathroom suites and velvet flock wallpaper were extremely quaint. Thank god I didn't have to look after Timmy again, that's all I can say.

After tea, I went to Dev's again to tell him how we'd got away with the Timmy **FiASCO**.

'Skill!' he said.

'SKULL, MORE LIKE!' I sniggered.

Then we fist bumped and I nearly broke my knuckle on his fake gold signet ring.

When we caught up with the party planning, I was even more excited to see how far along we'd got:

AGUNG'S 80TH BIRTHDAY PARTY
TO-DO LIST (6 days to go!)

- Guest list √

- Venue √

- Invitations √

- Food √

- Entertainment

- Presents

- Cake √

- Decorations √

There were only two jobs left to do – **HOORAY!** But Agung's *STRICTLY BALLROOM PRANCING* pressie still hadn't materialised. Looks like we're not going to be putting on our prancing shoes and PAAAARRRTTying anytime soon. I know there must be **kersquillions** of people begging Janine Jangle to pay them a visit, but our video was of such superior quality, I couldn't understand why she hadn't got back to us yet. Still, failing that, we had the eagle-shaped cake. And failing *that*, we had Dad's Cup Noodle maker. **ALL WAS NOT LOST.**

'So, entertainment is your area, Dev. How far have you got?' I said.

'Do you actually know what two pounds

fifty gets you these days?' he spat. 'Even Graham wouldn't fetch a stick for that!'

'ALL RIGHT, KEEP YOUR KNICKERS ON, MISSUS,' I said. 'What can we do for free, maybe a game of Pass the Parcel? That way I could wrap that abacus the Laus gave me and get rid of the blummin' thing.'

How to play FREE party games

Spork
Bath salts
Shoehorn

Wrap unwanted gifts for 'Pass the Parcel'

sniff

Blindfolded 'Find the Stilton Sandwich' game

Balloon Keepy Uppy

1001, 1002...

zzz

Balance stuff on Grandad

'What we need is your lucky coin,' said Dev.

The problem was, we were both **scared stiff** of the witch's house. Then I remembered how the coin wasn't just a lucky charm, it was a goldmine worth thousands. So even if the witch did turn us into a couple of warty-bummed toads or whatever, I'd have enough money to pay another witch to turn us back again. **SORTED.**

After explaining my **CUNNING** plan to Dev, we reluctantly returned to the scary house. We noticed that the hole in the railings had been cordoned off by the fire service, so climbing through the gap in the railings was definitely ruled out. Anyway, Mam had told us to apologise for the busted railings, so we had to speak to the owner no matter what. We played another

ROCK, PAPER, SCiSSORS to see which loser got to knock on the door this time. Twenty-seven games later, the sun had started going down. We had been trying our hardest to put off knocking and soon it would be dark enough for us to be dragged into the **evil hag's lair** without any of the neighbours noticing, never to be seen again! We decided on one last game, which I lost . . .

NOOOOOOOOO!!!

I got Dev to crouch behind a big plant pot by the side of the door, ready to call for help if needed, while I tapped the knocker. The footsteps inside got closer.

Then the key turned. This time, instead of legging it, I squeezed my eyes shut and prepared to meet my untimely death.

'Hello?' said a voice.

It didn't sound *demonic* and I couldn't feel bony fingers closing tightly around my throat, so I opened my eyes.

There was an ordinary lady in the doorway about the same age as Mam, armed with a duster, looking more scared of me than I was of her.

'**HI**,' I squeaked.

When I was sure the lady wasn't about to grab me and stuff me into a cauldron, I called

Dev over. Now the lady looked even more scared, but this time at Dev's **luminous pink fur gilet**. We told her about the railings and the COIN getting lost in her garden.

'Oh, I don't live here,' she said. 'I look after the house while the owner's away.'

OMG, SHE WAS THE HOUSEKEEPER! So, the lights turning on and off was her, even when the house seemed empty! Then I spotted the hoover in the hallway and that explained the ghostly **'woooo'** noises I had sometimes heard when I walked past.

'And the railings belong to the council, so they can fix that.' She waved us in. 'I'll let you through to the back so you can look for your COIN.'

She was ever so friendly, so we felt a bit silly thinking she'd been a witch all that time. However, I did keep my eyes open for bear traps, just to be sure. After a couple of minutes of poking about in the weeds, I found the coin. The string had caught on a twig so it was easily spotted.

'**MY PRECIOUS!**' I cried, kissing it like a long-lost puppy.

Dev screwed up his face and remarked, '**Eugh, you might want to wash that first.**'

I fixed the string with a quadruple knot, hung the coin back round my neck and tucked it safely under my jumper.

On the way back through the house, I had a good nose about. It was nothing like ours. We don't have oak panelling or fancy wallpaper.

177

We have dented skirting boards and ketchup smears. The dining room door was wide open so I did a quick snoop. It looked dead grand, with its crystal chandeliers, red velvet drapes and shiny mahogany floor. Perfect for Agung's party. **IF ONLY.**

That evening Dad made another one of his **'CLASSIC'** British dishes for tea – chicken tikka masala. The Laus didn't mind this time though. They'd already had their Britishness-fix with a pot of Earl Grey and clotted cream scones at the stately home.

The phone rang halfway through dinner and Mam picked up. She came back to the table all cheery. 'That was Eileen from Plunkthorpe Birders. They've chipped in and bought a birdwatching tour for Agung's birthday, and we're all invited. I know you haven't sorted a gift yet, Maddy, so that's great, isn't it?'

'Heh, yeah, brill,' I uttered feebly.

BLAST! That pressie was going to be way better than mine if Jangle didn't get her *bejewelled* backside into gear and respond soon. Dad told Agung about the tour bus and he clapped his hands with glee.

Later on, I heard Jack creeping to Kayla on his phone. I tiptoed up to his door and heard him persuading her to go on the birdwatching tour so that they could 'Get extra marks for the school conservation project.' *I'll* give him extra marks. Two black eyes if he carries on like that!

Monday

Even though the Laus are living their best lives staying at the four-star hotel at the **posh** end of town, I felt dead sorry for them today. They had planned on going to Sudmouth for a quintessential British seaside experience, but because it had been **BUCKETING IT DOWN** since last night, they had to cancel. They think they are missing out, but trudging around getting soaked to the bone IS the quintessential British seaside experience, if you ask me!

Unfortunately, it meant the Laus had to spend all day being miserable at our **MADHOUSE** instead.

I got back from school to find Mr and Mrs Lau sitting cowering on the sofa, while Ted and Tod, the **HUMAN TORNADOES**, destroyed every object around them. Timmy wasn't around. He was probably doing the smart thing and hiding upstairs with Oli.

SMASH!

SMASH!

Ted was treading a packet of custard creams into our (ex) new carpet while Tod was bashing in a Lego tower with a ladle. Mam tried to create 'calm the room energy' by lighting a lily scented candle but it didn't do anything apart from make the place **PONG**, so she put on a meditation music CD instead. The **EVIL TWINS** were screeching so loud, Mam had to turn it up to full volume to drown them out, so it had the opposite effect in the end.

I tried to cheer up the Laus with some friendly banter.

'YOU WANTED TO VISIT LONDON, DIDN'T YOU?' I shouted, gesturing around the room.

They nodded at me, confused.

'WELL, YOU'VE GOT PICCADILLY CIRCUS RIGHT HERE!'

I don't think they were very impressed.

I wanted to get away from the **GRUESOME TWOSOME** just as much as the Laus, so I resorted to self-preservation and left the room. I made the error of not retreating fast enough, because Mam stood in the doorway and said loudly, '**Maddy, keep an eye on the twins for two minutes while I get the clothes in the washer.**'

BRILLIANT.

When Mam says two minutes, she means two *centuries*. I was thinking of some excuse I hadn't used a billion times already, when **FUZZFACE** had one of her mad moments and attacked Mam's fluffy slippers as she walked past carrying a basket of laundry.

She tripped over the **WRETCHED MOGGY** and crashed to the floor, while the contents of the basket went flying out:

Oli's shorts,

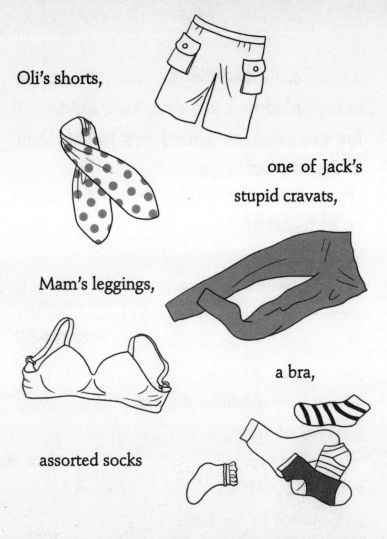

one of Jack's stupid cravats,

Mam's leggings,

a bra,

assorted socks

and a **pair of Dad's saggy Y-fronts**, which landed on Mrs Lau's perfectly coiffured hairdo.

Just as **FUZZFACE** scarpered out of the room, Agung walked in with Dad. Agung said something in Chinese, then Dad turned to Mam lying spreadeagled on the floor and remarked, **'Yeah, exactly what are my pants doing on Mrs Lau's head?'**

The twins stopped smashing the place up to laugh **HYSTERICALLY** at Mrs Lau's bulging eyes framed in each leg hole of the pants. Mam stumbled over to help her, but she was already peeling them off, while trying not to be sick. It was better than anything on the telly!

I gathered the dirty laundry while Mam apologised over the din of sitars twanging. I was pleased that *I* hadn't caused the **MAYHEM** for a change.

'Hey, Evil . . . I mean, Ted and Tod,' I said. 'If you come upstairs, I'll let you play with my . . . ' I thought desperately of a suitable lure, ' . . . ukulele.'

I DIDN'T HAVE A UKULELE.

'YAAY!' they yelled, running ahead.

HA! They fell for it, the dimwits.

How to FOOL dimwit toddlers

Look at this time machine!

Dimwits

(Actually a potato with chopsticks in it)

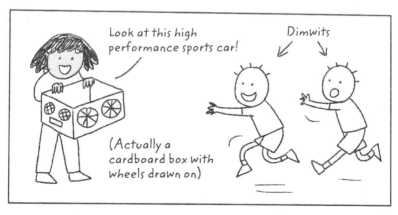

Look at this high performance sports car!

Dimwits

(Actually a cardboard box with wheels drawn on)

When I walked into my room, Oli was crouched down like a gorilla and Timmy was lying on the floor with his legs in the air.

'**RIGHT,**' I said. 'Are you going to tell me what's going on or what?'

'Nothing,' they both said, quickly getting up.

In Oli's world, *nothing* is always code word for *something*.

'Where uk-kra-lally?' asked Tod.

'WHAT'S A UK-KRA-LALLY?' said Oli.

I grabbed Oli's swing ball racket and started strumming it like a guitar.

'THIS, MY FINE FRIEND, IS A UKULELE.'

Oli and Timmy looked confused and were about to correct me when Ted screeched, 'Me want go!'

'No, me first!' yelled Tod.

I left them to fight amongst themselves while I called Dev to check on the Prancing situation. Agung's birthday was only five days away and Dev still had no luck. I could have lent him my COIN, but it was far too valuable. If he lost it, I would too – MY RAG, THAT IS!

'Don't worry about the pressie for now,' I said. 'Plunkthorpe Birders club have literally clubbed together and bought Agung a double-decker bus birdwatching trip.'

'Can I go on the birdwatching trip?' he asked.

'Don't be a NERD Dev, the only wings you're into are the ones on your batwing sleeved blouse.'

'**I know,**' he replied. 'But I need an excuse to wear my new hat.'

AMAZING.

I asked where he'd got to with the entertainment and Dev answered, 'I had this ace idea. We could get some modelling balloons with our two pounds fifty.'

I scoffed. 'And what, make a bunch of genetically mutated poodles?'

'Thanks for **BURSTING** my bubble,' sulked Dev.

'Sorry, but that idea did not go off with a **BANG**,' I quipped back.

I wanted to **EXPAND** on our balloon-related conversation, but the doorbell rang and I had to hang up to answer the door. It was Mr Tatlock coming to pick up his 'CHERUBS' as he calls them (IF ONLY HE KNEW). The Laus were nowhere to be seen. They had escaped while the coast was clear. Mam was in the kitchen nursing a sprained ankle with a bag of frozen organic falafels. I was secretly overjoyed, not about her injury, but the fact that she had ruined the falafels and we wouldn't be getting those disgusting things for dinner.

It had stopped raining at last so I went outside to find **FUZZFACE** to make sure she was all right. It must have been a shock to be suddenly buried under an avalanche of fusty undies. She wasn't in our garden so I peered over into Mr

Pike's. I needn't have worried. She was quite happily digging up his petunias and pooing on his ferns.

There was **crashing** about in the shed, so I went to see where Dad was up to with his Cup Noodle maker. As I opened the shed door, a jet of chilli sauce came spurting out of the machine and painted the outline of Australia over the front of my jumper. Then Dad wiped the sauce with an oily rag and turned the stain into the Outer Hebrides.

'As you can see, the machine's not quite a hundred per cent yet,' he said.

It is, I thought. **IT'S A HUNDRED PER CENT DEFECTIVE!**

As I went back into the house to change my jumper, I heard Jack on his phone. I tiptoed towards his door and listened in. 'So, you're coming to the party then? **Excellent!**' said Jack. 'I arranged for BAMBOO GARDEN to do an **exclusive** buffet menu. It's going to be top notch nosh.'

I rubbed the coin and waited for a **SNOT-FILLED METEORITE** to fall from the sky and splatter him, but nothing happened.

I still needed to get him back for being a **LYING BOZO**, and now was the time, so I called Dev for ideas. We are a highly imaginative team when it comes to taking revenge and within minutes came up with these **BEAUTIES**:

1. Hide his **Ninja Banana 2** game controller in Agung's pile of manure (horse not Agung's!)

2. Put permanent black paint around binocular eyepieces and tell him he can see Kayla's house from his bedroom with them

3. Glue one of **FUZZFACE**'s furballs onto the waxed bit of his monobrow while he is sleeping

4. Cut all the bum cheeks out of his **PANTS**

5. Replace his spot cream with squeezy cheese

6. Offer him a plasticine marshmallow, film it as he regurgitates, send film to Kayla

We were total and utter geniuses, or geneii, whatever the plural is. Although might bin numbers two and six, as they will require **OLYMPIC-LEVEL SPRINTING AWAY** skills and I run like I have two empty hot water bottles attached to my ankles instead of feet. I have stored the list safely in my bedside drawer until such time I feel brave enough to attempt one of them.

When the Laus came upstairs to collect Timmy, they informed us that they will be recuperating and making full use of their hotel relaxation facilities until the day of the party.

It is all right for some! Meanwhile, my relaxation will consist of:

1. Choking on Mam's stinking aromatherapy oils

2. Sticking wads of bog roll in my ears to drown out Mam's tuneless Tibetan chanting

3. Trying to unsee Mam demonstrating the *three-legged dog* yoga pose at every opportunity

Me, eighty!

Saturday morning - party day!!

Agung's birthday today!

It had been sopping wet and miserable all week, so the best party in Plunkthorpe for centuries had come at the perfect time. Everyone got back with their RSVPs in the end and they were all coming – **YAAAAAY!**

At ten o'clock, the bus arrived to take Agung on his birdwatching trip. It was ever so

IMPRESSIVE. It was a whole double-decker with pictures of falcons and kingfishers and other winged creatures I didn't know the names of on the side. On the front where the destination is usually displayed, it said **'Happy 80ᵗʰ Mr Yip'**. His birdwatching pals were already on board making a racket with their party blowers, which made sour-faced Pike from next door come out to **COMPLAIN**. He is only jealous because he will never have so much fun. The bus driver got off the bus with a young lad.

'Morning, revellers! I'm Patrick and this is my assistant Will.'

Will was a bit older than Jack, but with even more **spots** and **chin fluff**. He said, 'I'll be serving refreshments and answering any questions, as long as they aren't bird-, route- or bus-related.' And just like Jack, he was **enormously** helpful too.

Mam had fetched Timmy from his hotel earlier, so he got on board with Oli and Agung. Dev still hadn't shown up, so I ran over and knocked on his front door.

'**Sorry,**' he puffed, hurrying out. 'I couldn't make up my mind about the hat.'

I pointed out that he had a *deer*stalker on, when we were about to go *bird*watching.

'Yes, I know, but earflaps are so on trend right now,' he replied.

FANTASTIC.

Trendy

Lord save me

Just as Patrick started the engine, Jack turned up with Kayla, looking smarmy – **YUCK**. He was holding a clipboard and highlighter pen, trying to pretend that the trip was in aid of their school conservation project. I hope Kayla catches out the **CONNIVING CREEP** soon. Mam put him in charge, even though his management skills were non-existent. 'Make sure you get back for the party at **twelve on the dot!**' she ordered.

We waved to Mam and Dad as the bus pulled away. They were staying behind to get the drama club decorated. I was glad, as there were eighty giant balloons to blow up.

Some of the bus seats downstairs had been taken out to make way for a table full of reference books and **CRUSTY OLD** bird skulls. Agung and his pals crowded round it like they had discovered **TREASURE**. On the way to our first bird-spotting area, Will handed out croissants. I didn't get to taste a single crumb though, as the bus swerved to avoid a rabbit and the croissants shot off the tray and onto the floor. I did the 'three second rule' and went to pick one up before someone trod on it. A moment later, the bus veered again and chucked my lemon squash in my face. As I wiped the stinging liquid out of my eyes, I saw that everyone else was also trying to stop their drinks and croissants flying around.

ARGHH!

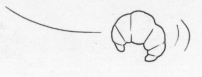

HOW TO EAT FOOD SECURELY

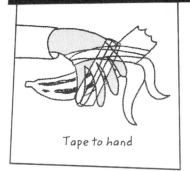

Tape to hand

Shove into gob in one go

DO NOT DISTURB

Build protective 'Scoffing Shelter'

Eat off a skewer

Kayla opened a window and stuck her face out for some fresh air. Jack tried to take her mind off being **queasy** by showing her a crow skull and she went even more green. Me and Dev suspected she had travel sickness. Either that, or she was sick of Jack – **HA HA!**

Patrick stopped the bus so we could get off and let Will mop up the **MESS**. Agung and his pals, being experienced birdwatchers, had come prepared. They got out their packed lunches and started tucking in – they weren't going to starve! A minute later, it started chucking it down. Jack tried to shield Kayla with a croissant tray, but just succeeded in tipping a pile of greasy crumbs on her head. Me and Dev had planned to take revenge on Jack, but he was doing an **amazing** job making a **DORK** of himself all on his own!

We continued our trip around the countryside, but there wasn't a single bird around. Probably because they were sitting on their lovely dry nests, laughing at us **STUPID HUMANS**. Oli and Timmy were banging about on the top deck so

I went to shut them up. As I stomped upstairs, I noticed something through the steamed-up front window resembling a huge bird. I shouted excitedly to the birders downstairs. **'HEY, THERE'S AN EMU OUTSIDE!'**

'Don't be a wassock,' someone shouted back.

CHARMING.

'They're not native,' someone else bellowed.

I wiped the window and looked again. They were right, it wasn't an emu. It was a woman wearing a *flouncy feather boa*. She was with three other people, waving by a van on the roadside. Patrick slowed the bus and pulled over. He got out and dad-jogged over to see what the **PROBLEM** was. It looked like their van had broken down. Patrick pointed to the bus and they came our way. Me and the **BRATS** scrambled downstairs to check out the most excitement we'd had all day.

The flustered, soaked strangers said 'Hi' to us all and sat down, while Will handed them tea towels to dry off with. The woman with the boa looked vaguely familiar, then Dev suddenly screamed, **'OH MY GOD, IT'S JANINE JANGLE, FROM STRICTLY BALLROOM PRANCING!'**

Everyone turned and stared. It was hard to tell as her hair was stuck to her face and mascara was running down her cheeks. Not her normal pristine self.

'Oh, watch out, Einstein's on board!' the woman spouted, in a high-pitched voice. She flashed a toothy smile and pointed to Dev with her crimson false nail.

There was no mistake. **It WAS Janine Jangle!**

'**My beehive's ruined**, but nothing a pina colada wouldn't sort. Do they serve those here?' Janine asked Dev, who was so **starstruck** he was almost sitting on her lap.

I dragged Agung over and pointed at her. **'LOOK WHO IT IS!'** I squealed.

He recognised her straight away, which is a miracle for him. **'Oh!'** he exclaimed, followed by a barrage of excited sounding Chinese. **'You dance TV!'** He did some swaying movements, as if trying to do the foxtrot with just his arms, then gave her a big hug. Agung can be so cute when he's not ***BURPING*** . . . or ***FARTING*** . . . or ***SNORING***.

'This is my grandad, your **BIGGEST** fan and he **LOVES** dancing,' I spluttered.

'BUT HE'S GOT ONIONS,' said Oli.

'BUNIONS,' I corrected.

'You don't have to tell me who this is,' said Janine, opening a compact mirror and applying pearly pink lipstick. 'I know who he is, because I know who you are.'

She pointed at her three friends, as everyone listened in.

'This is my **fabulous** TV crew. Zoe the producer, Yosef the camera guy and Leo, sound. And we were all blown away by your Surprise a Prancer video.'

ZOE   YOSEF   LEO

WHAAATTTTT??!!!

'We were on our way to yours when our van conked out,' said Zoe.

O.M.G.

'But . . . but we never got a reply to our email,' I said.

'We sent it last week,' Yosef replied.

'It might have ended up in my mam's junk mail,' said Dev. 'She never checks that.'

UGH, THAT'LL BE WHY THEN.

Janine cleared a space on the table. 'Well, don't you worry your pretty little noggins, because I, the one and only **Mizz Jangle**, am gracing you with my presence now!'

She swept her boa **theatrically** around her neck, tottered onto the table in her heels, then clapped to hush everyone. 'I've never **Surprised a Prancer** on a bus before. But I have to say it's hands down the most **glamorous** location so far!'

Everyone laughed.

'Anyhow, today's all about Agung and we're here to have fun, so it's time to put on your **prancing** shoes and . . . what's it time for?' she cupped a hand to her ear and leaned forward.

'PAAAARRRTTY!!' we all

shouted.

Dev did a double pirouette ending in a moonwalk, hoping she would hire him as a **Star Prancer** on the spot. Agung did his shoulder jiggle and everyone else cheered and blew their party blowers. Wow, I couldn't believe we'd actually pulled it off!

Patrick got on the bus, oblivious to the **CELEBRATiON** and said to Janine and her crew, 'Your van's got a flat tyre. I can take you into town rather than you wait for the breakdown truck out here. Plunkthorpe's not far.'

Patrick didn't have a clue who Janine was. He was more of a TV darts fan, I think.

'Yes, I know where I am, my luv,' she replied. 'I've got a holiday home in town cos that's where I was brought up. You won't have recognised me when I've been about up here though, cos I wear me other **wig**.' Then she turned to the rest of us and said, 'Eeeh, it's dead nice to come back and pay tribute to my hometown, you know. Cos I wouldn't be who I am today without Plunkthorpe.'

'I always thought she had a Plunkthorpe accent,' Kayla whispered to Jack.

'Anyway, less talk, more Prancing. We've got a party to go to!' said Janine, getting off the table and nudging Patrick to his driver's seat.

'AND A CHINESE BLANKET!' said Oli.

I rolled my eyes. **'BANQUET.'**

Janine winked. 'Talking of blankets, will I get to see Agung's duvet cover with my face printed on it?'

Oh no, she mustn't find out it was just a tea stain. 'It's . . . at the dry cleaners,' I replied. **PHEW, THAT WAS CLOSE!**

Saturday - afternoon

W.O.W.

Me and Dev could NOT believe that we'd bagged Janine Jangle for Agung's party after all – it must have been the lucky coin working its *magic*!

On the way back, everyone soon forgot about the birdwatching when Janine started telling her *sensational* behind-the-scenes stories!

'Yosef ended up in casualty when I did a high kick and my **stiletto** flew off and hit him straight in the bonce!' she roared.

'We've had to Sellotape her shoes on ever since,' Yosef said.

'I had to get my head cut out of railings,' said Timmy. **'But I only have a bruise.'**

Janine **screeched** and nearly fell off her chair laughing. Agung could hardly understand a word, but giggled along because he was so happy. Jack tried to call Mam to tell her we were running late, but she wasn't answering.

Half an hour later, the bus parked outside

the drama club. There was a scrum as everyone elbowed each other out of the way to see if the Chinese buffet was ready yet. Funny how easily a **celebrity** is forgotten about when free grub is on offer!

Me and Dev chaperoned Janine into the building. Everything had turned out perfectly. All those weeks of planning and stressing had paid off, and now Janine Jangle was here, in the flesh! We'd be **LOCAL LEGENDS**, the press would be clamouring for interviews, we'd be all over the news. The venue was bound to look **FANTASTIC** too, as Mam, Dad and Miss Gabb had been decorating all morning.

'TA-DAAAAA!!' I chirped, walking in first with a wave of my hand.

Dev and Janine's faces fell.

I looked around.

WHAT THE?

The room was no different apart from a single **You Are Eighty Matey!** poster I'd made and three shrivelled balloons hanging off the lightshade. My parents and Miss Gabb were standing in a massive puddle in the middle of the room, wearing wellies and holding mops, while everyone else stood about looking **SHOCKED**.

'WHAT . . . HAPPENED?' I gasped.

Miss Gabb pointed at a wet patch in the ceiling. 'The roof's leaking. **Badly**.'

The money that me and Dev raised to keep the club open obviously hadn't stretched to roof repairs. **I SOBBED INSIDE.**

Then Mam cried out, 'Is that . . . ?!' She hobbled over (her ankle was still swollen after she faceplanted the other day) and gawped at Janine's face. 'It IS you!'

Janine zhuzhed her damp beehive and answered, 'Reminder appreciated.'

Dad sploshed over too and said, 'You're that Janine Jangle off the telly.'

'I know, isn't it COOL?' me and Dev squealed.

Miss Gabb curtsied. 'It's an honour to have such an acclaimed celebrity in my humble premises,' she gushed.

'Shame that's "dampened" the day,' Janine joked, eyeing the puddle.

'Does that mean the party's off then?' asked Dev.

'NOOOO,' I wailed, dropping to my knees and hammering the floor with my fists.

Dev quickly stopped me when he realised I was splashing dirty water over his new hat.

There was nothing left to do but rub my lucky coin.

And that's when Janine piped up, 'Panic over, people! My house is only down the road. We can have the party there.'

NO. WAY.

THE COIN WORKED! I was so relieved I forgot where I was for a moment and shouted out, '**I LOVE YOU, I DO!**'

We immediately went about packing up the party stuff and carried it to Janine's, using the Viking shields, sombreros and superhero capes from the drama club prop cupboard as umbrellas.

How to use alternative brollies

Viking shield

Sombrero

Superhero cape

✓

Postage stamp

Sieve

Candy floss

✗

Miss Gabb wrote the new venue address on a sign and stuck it to the drama club door for the guests who hadn't arrived yet.

After a short trek, Janine stopped and opened a gate. **'Welcome to my humble residence!'**

I glanced up at the entrance and nearly had a heart attack. It was none other than . . .

THE WITCH'S HOUSE!

Except it wasn't. It was the home of real-life, *A-list celebrity*, Janine Jangle!

I wondered if she knew it was us who ruined her railings. I didn't want to bring it up so I kept quiet and hoped her housekeeper wasn't in. Janine led us into the **huge** dining room and helped us push the table and chairs to one side to make even more space. While everyone took in the **swish** furnishings, *twinkling* chandeliers and *glossy* floor, Mam drove off to pay for and collect the birthday cake from the baker's.

I whispered to Dev. 'When we were last here, I was wishing the party could be in this very dining room – and now it is.'

'Magic,' mouthed Dev, pointing to the coin around my neck.

Not long after, the Sharmas arrived, then Mr and Mrs Lau, followed by the Tatlocks with their **OBNOXIOUS OFFSPRING**. They **'Oohed'** at the spectacular room, **'Ahhed'** at the decorations and then **'Eeekkked!'** when they realised who the unexpected host was. When Dad explained to the Laus about Janine's *celebrity status*, Mr Lau got out his camera and started frantically taking pictures.

'Janine must be like royalty,' remarked Mrs Lau, staring up at the ceiling. 'These chandeliers are bigger than the ones we saw at the stately home we visited the other day!'

I said to them, 'And you thought you weren't going to meet anyone famous around here.'

Then Mr Pike arrived. Dad told me he had to invite him, as he was threatening to complain to the council about the noise on the bus this morning. **WHAT A MISER!**

Now all the guests were here, Janine dinged a glass. Somehow, she had managed to swap her wig, slap on a fresh load of make-up and change into a **slinky dress** without us even noticing. **NOW THAT'S WHAT I CALL A PRO!**

'If you can't beat the rain, join it,' she shrilled. 'Look, I've put my **mermaid-cut gown** on, ready for a paddle!'

Everyone applauded with delight.

'Now as Agung, our birthday boy, is a big fan of **STRICTLY BALLROOM PRANCING**, I thought, why not recreate it, right here, in this very room?'

More cheers.

'Thought you'd be up for that,' Janine grinned. 'So, what are we waiting for? **'It's time to put on your prancing shoes and PAAAARRRTTY!!'**

YESSS! Now the entertainment was sorted too – **RESULT!**

Dad explained to Agung what was happening and he clapped.

'This is brilliant!' I heard Kayla whisper to Jack.

HUH? This party was all my doing, but she still thought it was all down to him! Tomorrow will be revenge day, starting with number three on my WAYS TO MAKE JACK PAY list: glue one of **FUZZFACE**'s furballs onto the waxed bit of his monobrow while he is sleeping.

The TV crew got ready to film. Yosef positioned his camera and Leo held the boom microphone over Janine. Zoe switched on some music and called out, **'We need volunteers to get up on this dance floor.'**

Dev's hand shot up like a rocket. **WHAT A SURPRISE.** Margot and Fred from the birdwatching club offered to do a waltz and Jack and Kayla wanted to do a scene from the film *Grease*. (Didn't Jack already do a grease scene after tipping croissant crumbs over Kayla's head earlier? **HA HA!**). Oli and Timmy put their hands up too. I had no idea what those two **CLOWNS** were up to, but at least I'd get a laugh out of it.

Yosef started the camera rolling and yelled, **'Action!'**

Janine stepped into the middle of the dance floor.

Come on, take the plunge!

'Welcome to another glitz-filled episode of Britain's favourite dance competition, **STRICTLY BALLROOM PRANCING**, with me, your host, Janine Jangle. First up, give a big hand to Margot and Fred with their waltz!'

They were surprisingly agile considering they both had walking boots on. But Fred's laces were undone and he tripped and **twinged** his false knee, so they had to abandon the dance early.

Jack and Kayla were up next. I can't say much about their rendition of 'You're the One That I Want', because I locked myself in the loo until I knew it was safe to come out again.

Then it was Dev's turn. He must have dashed home because he *sashayed* in wearing a *studded gold onesie* I'd not seen before.

He did a body pop and said, 'Now watch as I blow your mind!'

With that, he **JITTERBUGGED** on, but slid on a *diamanté jewel* that had fallen off his trouser leg and crashed into Ted and Tod, toppling them over like a couple of skittles!

WAAAHH!

OOOOF!

Saturday - evening

Zoe had to stop the music and check everyone for injuries, but Dev wouldn't get off the dance floor. In the end, Mrs Sharma had to intervene and drag him off by his ear. The **EVIL TWINS** weren't dead as I'd hoped. They were up and about within seconds, tearing the place apart, **WORST LUCK**.

Dev was **MORTIFIED** about his moment of glory being ruined.

'I'll never be **Star Prancer** now!' he bawled.

'Calm down, you've not even left school yet,' I said.

'School's for losers!' he sobbed, wiping his **SNOT** on my sleeve.

'Don't knock it. School might just teach you how to glue **diamantés** on properly . . . and also how to use tissues.'

I grimaced, wiping his **SNOT** back onto his sleeve.

Oli and Timmy were about to come on and we were so intrigued, Dev stopped **WHINGING** immediately. I couldn't wait to watch the disaster unfold. But instead of a complete load of dross, they did the most superb gymnastics routine I have ever seen in real life, with forward rolls, cartwheels and even a (dodgy) back flip. To top it off right at the end, Oli looped his arms over his head and bowed his legs, making an **'eight'** shape and Timmy laid on his belly and clutched his ankles from behind to make a **'zero'**.

'**Me, eighty!**' Agung said, pointing to himself. And everyone else gave them a standing ovation.

So *that* was the **SECRET WEIRD STUFF** they'd been doing together: Timmy had been teaching Oli how to do gymnastics – **NICE ONE!** Janine *swished* onto the dance floor in a lace hoop skirt and Elizabethan ruff. I didn't think it was possible but she easily beat Dev in the **OUTLANDISH** outfit stakes.

'**Time to announce the winners!**' she said. The room went quiet. 'They **FLABBERGASTED US** with their flips, **BOWLED US OVER** with their rolling and **CAPTIVATED US** with their cartwheels. They are of course, Oli and Timmyyyyy!'

They won the competition by miles. In fact, it was a complete *walkover*!

The amateur acrobats ran over to collect their **prizes**, which were just a couple of plastic medals from the drama club prop box, but by the looks on their faces, they might as well have been the real deal.

'And just because you're such a **TALENTED BUNCH**,' Janine continued. 'I want to make sure we get more of us Plunkthorpian stars out there. So, I'm giving Miss Gabb a grant to get the drama roof fixed!'

Everyone **congratulated** Miss Gabb and

crowded onto the dance floor as Zoe started the music again. Agung toddled up to Janine and motioned for a dance.

'Oh hello, the expert's going to show us how it's done!' said Janine, chuckling.

Agung did his jiggle and Janine copied.

Jiggle Jiggle

Is very hao gow

'Hao gow!'

he said.

'What's that mean when it's at home?' Janine replied.

'THAT MEANS SO MUCH FUN,' said
Oli, getting it right for once.

'Well, in that case, I'm really having hao gow!'
said Janine, **shimmying** her shoulders.

How to do the 'Agung Shoulder Jiggle'

Jiggle right shoulder
two times

Jiggle left shoulder
two times

Jiggle both shoulders
three times

...all while hands are turning
an invisible door knob

Everyone joined in, including Mam, who had just returned from the baker's with the birthday cake. She had to stop after Dad spun her around too vigorously and made her sprained ankle throb again. She was gutted she missed Oli and Timmy's gymnastics, but they promised to show her later.

The Chans must have been **MiND READERS** because they came in with the food just at the right moment. Apart from the birders, who had **SCOFFED** their packed lunches this morning, the rest of us were ready to gnaw our own arms off. We pushed the chairs and table back into the middle of the room, and as soon as the Chans finished laying out the buffet, everyone **descended like piranhas**. At that rate, I was probably going to be left with one chopstick and **CLAMMY LEFTOVERS**. Party organising is a thankless job! Even Mr Pike pushed in front of me, the **CHEEKY BEGGAR**. Better him than Ged Sponger though. I was glad he hadn't turned up after nabbing Dev's invite.

After the buffet, Mam said some thank yous.

'Firstly, to the Chans for providing the amazing spread!'

The Chans looked pleased because they had gained a load of new customers.

'To the **gorgeous** Janine, for hosting. I think we've all gone past your home at some point and wondered what it was like inside. We're not disappointed, I can tell you that.'

ESPECIALLY ME, WHEN I FOUND OUT THE OWNER WASN'T A WITCH!

'And last but not least, Maddy and Dev, for putting this whole event together.'

Everyone whooped. Apart from Kayla, who was standing at the back of the room with her hands on her hips, scowling at Jack. Just as the noise died down, we heard her shout, **'I thought you said you'd organised everything?!'**

Jack went red and skulked out of the room. **HA!** Maybe I don't need to take revenge after all. That was just as humiliating as having a furball glued to your face as far I was concerned!

Mam carried on. 'Now let's all sing "Happy Birthday" to Agung and cut the cake!'

She walked over to the sealed box, ready to do a **BiG REVEAL**. I couldn't wait to see Agung's face. How could he not be delighted at the truly **magnificent** eagle-shaped confection?

'Happy birthday to yooouuuuuu!' We all sang the last line of the song as Mam cut the ribbon on the box. She lifted the lid, and we all leaned in to coo at it.

'WHY'S IT GOT . . . FOUR LEGS?!' I
cried, not recognising the shape as any bird of
prey I've ever seen.

Dev turned to me and blared, **'That's not
an eagle. That's a beagle!'**

IT WAS A FLIPPING DOG, NOT A BIRD! Nobody knew whether to laugh or feel sorry for me, so there was just awkward silence.

'THEY MUST HAVE GIVEN YOU THE WRONG CAKE,' I complained to Mam.

Mam checked the receipt and confirmed it was ours.

GREAT.

The **DITZY** baker lady must have misheard over the noise in the shop that day. I explained to everyone what I thought had happened and they cracked up in hysterics. There was no sympathy. Glad the entertainment was going well, on my account.

'**Maybe the baker was barking mad,**' said Janine, trying to make me feel better.

'**Well, it all goes down the same hole,**' said Dad, making me feel worse.

At this point, still not knowing it was meant to be an eagle, Agung came over, pointed to the cake and said, '**Hao liang.**' I know that means 'very nice', and I know that dogs are his favourite animals after birds, **FUZZFACE** and frill-necked lizards, so that made up for the glaring error.

Mam cut the cake and handed it around. It had loads of butter icing and tasted **LUSH**, so in the end it didn't matter what shape it was. Jack gave the beagle's shiny nose to Kayla as a peace offering and it made her giggle. I suppose that means he is back in her good books now – **JAMMY GIT.**

After the cake, Agung opened his presents. He got:

• A cagoule

• A bird print lanyard to hold his specs **(WHICH I GUARANTEE HE WILL NEVER USE)**

• A box of **SPECIAL** edition sage and onion stuffing flavour Cup Noodles

• One night's stay at the Plunkthorpe Park Hotel from the Laus. I think they felt sorry for him having to sleep on his **LUMPY** mattress in the garage, but he is not bothered in the least

Dad's gift was in the car boot. He took Agung outside to see it and all the guests followed. I already knew about his portable Cup Noodle maker, so I stood at the back of the crowd while Dad demonstrated his invention. A few seconds later, Dev yanked my sleeve. **'Don't look now but plonker's here.'**

Ged marched over and grunted, **'Where's the grub?'**

'You're too late, it's all gone,' I said, smugly.

'So's this,' he snorted, grabbing the string around my neck with my lucky coin on. I didn't want to lose it again after the nightmare of getting back last time, so I stamped on his foot.

256

'**OW!**' he yelled.

Everyone turned to see what the noise was, just as Agung was pushing a button on Dad's machine. The contraption **whirred** and a spout popped out, **SQUIRTING** red hot chilli sauce right into Ged's ugly mug. Dad had clearly forgotten about fixing that faulty component.

'**AGHHH!!**'

Ged screamed, clutching his face.

'**Here, let me help, luv,**' said Janine, switching on her garden hose and blasting it at Ged, soaking him through.

'**ARGH ... NO!**' he cried, stumbling off.

Then we all stared in wonder as he lolloped across the road, tripped over a kerb, **BOUNCED** off a lamp post and **CRASHED** headlong into a rhododendron.

HA, HA, HA!

'I saw that **good-for-nowt** trying to steal off you,' said Janine, winking at me.

I was going to have to go into hiding for a very long time after this, but it was worth it.

After Mam extracted Ged from the bush, made sure he wasn't scarred by the chilli and sent him packing, we went inside and cleared up. Of course, Mr Pike had conveniently left by then. I wish the **EVIL TWINS** had too, instead of going around popping balloons and treading in leftover cake while we were trying to put stuff away.

Janine did a mini house tour for the Laus and anyone else who wanted, then changed into a scarlet **frilled** flamenco dress and let us take a billion selfies with her. She gave Dev her **feather boa** and told him he had **Star Prancer** potential, which meant that in every single photo he had taken with her, he is ugly happy crying. As we were leaving, Janine said, 'Watch out for your **Surprise a Prancer** clip on the telly in a few weeks.'

'YOU BET WE WILL!' I replied, peeling Agung's fingers off her door frame. He didn't want to go, bless him.

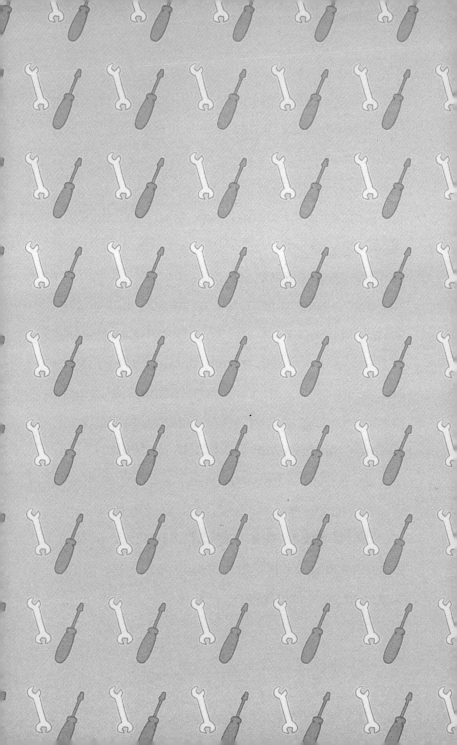

Sunday

I've lost count of the messages I've got today telling me how **SUPERB** yesterday's party was. Well, it was always my intention to make it go down in Plunkthorpe history. Plus, me and Dev are PDA (Pretty Darned Awesomesauceness). Now the party's over with, I can chill out at last!

I was ready to take a few relaxation tips from Mam, so I went to see if she could teach me a few yoga poses. It smelled of smoke as I was going downstairs and thought she might be burning some of Agung's joss sticks. But when I walked into the living room, I found Mam **FRANTICALLY** beating a cushion against the curtain, which had burst into flames. Dad pushed past me with a bucket of water and chucked it on the fire. We stood back as it **sizzled** and went out.

'WHAT HAPPENED?!' I coughed, wafting smoke out of my eyes.

SPLOSH!

cough!
splutter!

'MAM SET FIRE TO THE CURTAINS WITH HER COMA THERAPY CANDLES!'

shouted Oli, like the world was about to end.

'YOU MEAN, AROMATHERAPY,' I said.

Although we *could* have ended up in a coma, passing out in those fumes.

'Nearly had to call out Plunkthorpe fire services again,' Dad chuckled, nervously.

Mam looked sheepish. 'It's actually **stressing me out**, all this candle-lighting, head-standing, room-spraying, Tibetan chanting, facepack-making, meditation music-playing nonsense. I think I'll go back to punching things.'

After all that, Mam's going back to boxing at the gym? So much for the calming advice!

We opened all the doors and windows to air the house before the Laus came for lunch for the last time. Dad made cheese and pickle sandwiches, which is *my* favourite classic British dish. The Laus were flying back to Hong Kong today and were trying to work out how to cram fourteen teapots and twenty-five Union Jack tea towels into their luggage.

'We're taking lots of lovely memories back with us,' said Mrs Lau.

Apart from being terrorised by the **EVIL TWINS**, I'm sure.

'This is the BEST souvenir of all though,' said Mr Lau, holding up his phone. He then proceeded to scroll through his photos and took so long showing us every one of his hundred and thirty-four selfies with his wife and Janine Jangle, I thought they were going to miss their plane.

Oli and Timmy demonstrated their gymnastic routine in the garden so Mam could finally see it. It was even better than before, with extra (dodgy) backflips! Agung grinned and pointed to himself again when they finished with the **eight zero** sign made in limb form.

ELEVEN

SEVEN

SIX

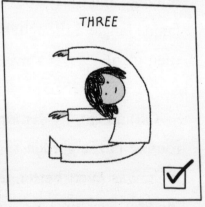

THREE

The best bit for me though was when **FUZZFACE** got so dizzy watching she threw up on Jack's shoe **(HE, HE)**.

266

Oli and Timmy were
a bit sad knowing they
weren't going to see
each other again for
ages, so I took a group
picture of them, wearing
their plastic gold medals and posing with the
medieval knight, and the new addition, Grogu.

When the **posh** taxi arrived to take them
back to Plunkthorpe Park Hotel to pick up
their things, we said our goodbyes and hugged.
Agung went on for ages in Chinese to them and
Dad told us he was just making sure they brought
pak choi next time they visited. Dad said that
Agung could always fly to Hong Kong and visit
them, but Mam said he couldn't manage such a
long flight with his sciatica.

As we waved from our doorstep, I noticed Oli's bottom lip only wobbled slightly. He has matured a lot since making friends with Timmy. I wish Jack would mature.

Seeing the **posh** taxi again reminded me how well-off the Laus were and then I remembered . . . it was time to cash in my lucky Chinese coin! I went to my room and called Dev and we listed off all the things we were going to buy **immediately**:

- The entire stock of the **NINETY-NINE PENCE SHOP** (me and Dev)

- One night at Plunkthorpe Park Hotel to sample the free honey roasted cashews **(me and Dev)**

- A wardrobe of designer sequinned hot pants in every colour **(Dev)**

- Crystal chandelier earrings **(Dev)**

- A house with a separate bedroom for Oli and a proper bedroom (not garage) for Agung **(me)**

- A one-way ticket to Outer Mongolia for Ged **(me and Dev)**

After we had agreed that these were extremely well-thought-out, sensible purchases, I hung up and went to find Dad. He was in the kitchen fiddling with the faulty chilli sauce nozzle on his Cup Noodle maker, while the rest of the family argued over what was wrong with it. I barged in and handed Dad my coin.

'Dad, can you ask Agung where he got this from? It might help me find out how much it's worth,' I said.

He took it off me, showed it to Agung and said something in Chinese. Agung examined it for precisely one second and answered briefly. Dad gave the coin back to me and said, 'It came off one of them things you hang on the car mirror.'

'WHAT, A PIDDLY CHEAPO TRINKET?'

I spluttered. **'NO, THAT CAN'T BE RIGHT!'**

Jack cracked up. **'You're rich, whoopie.'**

Agung said something else.

'Oh no, he got that wrong,' Dad corrected.

PHEW.

'He said it could have fallen off a keyring too.'

NOOOOOOO!!!!

I gawped at the COin. 'But he made out it was **DEAD VALUABLE**. He said the words "hao dor" which you told me means "a lot"!' I wailed.

Dad shrugged and said something to Agung again. Agung belly laughed and replied.

'Ah,' said Dad, nodding. 'He said he had "a lot" of these coins cluttering up his room and was trying to get rid of them.'

EXCELLENT.

SO, I'M NOT GOING TO BE RICH. Anyway,

who am I kidding? Hardly anyone becomes a **millionaire** overnight by doing nowt. Dad always tells me you need to work at being successful, like he does, so that's what I'll do . . . and who knows, I could be the best party planner the world has ever known!

The end

MADDY YIP'S

GUIDE TO LIFE

STORY and PICTURES by Sue Cheung

My name is **Maddy Yip**. I live with my two annoying brothers, mum, dad and Agung (my Chinese grandad). My BEZZIE, Dev, lives two doors down. GUESS WHAT? Everyone has a talent except for ME! So now I'm going to find my **life's calling** – even if it means rubbish recorder-playing, **bad** breakdancing, worse baking, and losing the school **guinea pig** along the way. Surely I'm good at something other than **armpit farts**?

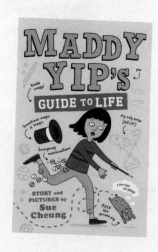

'Hilarious' *Guardian*

'The laughs come thick and fast' *LoveReading*

MADDY YIP'S

GUIDE TO HOLIDAYS

STORY and PICTURES by Sue Cheung

My name is **Maddy Yip**. I'm off on a seaside holiday with my bezzie Dev. Our biggest **dream** is to ride on the brand new, completely **mind-blowing** roller coaster called the MEGA BEAST! One problem though: I have to bring my annoying little brother and my **bonkers** grandad along for the weekend. I mean, dealing with **killer seagulls** is bad enough! Will they stop me from loop-the-looping on the BEST RIDE EVER?

'Another laugh-out-loud excursion into the madcap world of Maddy Yip'
LoveReading